Secrets of Zynpagua

Return of the Princess

Ilika Ranjan

PARTRIDGE

A Penguin Random House Company

For my wonderful parents, angels of my life, who
have made my world a lovely fairytale.

"Let your mind start a journey through a strange new world. Leave all thoughts of the world you knew before. Let your soul take you where you long to be... Close your eyes, let your spirit start to soar, and you'll live as you've never lived before."

- **Erich Fromm**, psychologist & philosopher.

Acknowledgement

Little did I know that the heavens above would send messengers, disguised in many forms, to support me in this arduous journey to become an author.

I am very grateful to the following people for helping me live my dreams.

My lovely sisters, Malvika and Geetika, for cushioning my life and filling it with every possible hope and luxury. For their relentless chanting of 'Nam Myo Ho Renge Kyo' to make my dreams come true.

My friend Nirupama Rao, for always believing in me and standing by me.
She titled my first book 'Puppet on the fast track'

My friend Swati Kapoor Malhotra, for being a wonderful human being. Her persistent attempt in reaching out to people for my book has been an inspiration, filling my mind with so much positivity. Her sweet daughter Aarna Malhotra reminds me of the character Anika in the book.

My friend Mona Dhaliwal for her prayers, care and support. A truly loving human being.

My friend Amrita Kanhere for her constant reinforcement of my belief in Sai Baba. I continue to nag her with my mundane problems and she continues to listen to me patiently.

My friend Bhavna Vats for her confidence in my future. Her newly acquired astrological skills resonate east or west, the results are going to be the best.

My friend Richa Singh for bringing back all the school memories. I especially thank her for painting Vivian's house in Zynpagua (The picture is in the book).

My friends Shweta Thakur and Meetu Thakur. A special thank you to Meetu for painting the scenery of Zynpagua for me.

My friend Shilpi Sen for literally drilling and killing the critics of my work.

My friend Nithya Ranganathan for her constant motivation and encouragement.

My Wassup chat group - Smriti Mehra, Mansi Shukla, Swati Malhotra, Richa Singh for filling my life with humour and giggles.

My Friends Vani Gupta and Boski for always trying to help and support.

My friend Aparna Gupta for her patience and being the first to buy my book.

My senior in Citibank, Sanjeev Moghe, for his persistent encouragement for both my entrepreneurial venture and book writing. I am also grateful to his wife Shilpa Moghe for sharing the passion for travel with me.

My friend Nikhel Goel, for constantly appreciating my work.

Suresh Menon for his outstanding support in reaching out to people for my first book Puppet on the Fast Track and for always being very helpful and kind.

The Initiators of the journey

I extend my sincerest gratitude to Pranav Kumar from IMA-India for giving me a chance to write my first travelogue for their magazine CFO connect.

My friend Anshul Arora, for pushing me to write, for recommending my book *Puppet on the Fast track* to his friends in media. His little daughter-Arainna Arora, happens to be the youngest member of my reading club.

Leadstart Publishing: the publishers of my first book *Puppet On The Fast Track*. A wonderful and humble team who helped me understand the nitty gritty of book publishing.

Heritage School of Languages - run by Brazilian gentleman Rauni and his British wife Betty in Lucknow.

I could not have learnt Spanish if the institute did not hold special classes for me, for two years, compensating for my perpetual absence from Lucknow. A big thank you to my teachers and friends Otoniel, Rebecca, Marsio and Carol for making learning of Spanish so easy and enjoyable.

Authors

Vikram Sampath, the author of *Splendours of Royal Mysore: the untold story of the Wodeyars, Voice of Veena, My name is Gauhar Jaan*. I am thankful to him for his patient listening and candid advice on promoting a children fiction.

I owe a big thank you to my childhood friend Swati Malhotra for making me speak to him.

Jashodhara Lal, the author of *Just Married, Please excuse* and *Sorting out Sid-* for her suggestions on submitting manuscripts, for sharing her submissions. I am grateful to my friend Vani Gupta for introducing me to her.

Motivators-

I extend my sincerest gratitude to Mr Achal Paul, Director of Buzzcomm, for being very kind and approachable, for his patient listening of my expectations and sharing his perspective on book promotion. He updated me on the latest trends being followed and has been offering very practical and logical advice for making this book a success.

Himangini Babla, the owner of Spellbound, the kid's bookstore in Mumbai. A genteel and compassionate woman, who feels so strongly about promoting reading amongst children. Her determination to recommend only quality books for children is very motivating and worth appreciating.

Rashmi Binani
A very positive and accurate astrologer who has helped me understand the functioning of stars in my life.

Ladakh- Heavens have descended here! The tall snowcapped Himalayan ranges can push anyone to clear the cobwebs in the mind and start thinking afresh. I owe a big thank you to Mr Ajaz Radhu and Tsomori travels for introducing this marvelous destination to me.

The creative team of Secrets of Zynpagua:
Return of the Princess

I have been constantly thanking God for making me meet these creative individuals who have garnished my book Secrets of Zynpagua: Return of the Princess with wonderful sketches, paintings, beautiful music and song.

Thank you very much my dear team-

Nideep Varghese- one of the most talented and humble artists I have ever met. His sketches of Anika, Vivian, Drudan, Femina, Sussaina, Leo and Frederick, have filled so much life in the book.

The cover page of this book is a testimony of his outstanding talent and creativity.

Richa Singh, a wonderful painter, for painting Vivian's house, especially on my request.

Meetu Thakur, an extremely talented person, for painting the scenery of life in Zynpagua.

Achint Khare: A very versatile musician and composer. I had not imagined that he would create such a melodious and attractive music for the title song of *Secrets of Zynpagua: Return of the Princess.*

Aditi Veena for lending her melodious voice for the title song of Secrets of Zynpagua: Return of the Princess.

Their work can also be seen and heard on: https://www.facebook.com/pages/Secrets-of-Zynpagua-Return-of-the-Princess

Jaishree Sethi- the Creative Director of Story Ghar. I thank her for encouraging reading amongst children and introducing a unique and musical concept of story telling.

Beta Soft Technology: for designing my blog, for suggesting innumerable ways of reaching out and always being very prompt and professional. I am very grateful to Manish Khandelwal and his team for their technological backup.

Ann Minoza from Patridge publishing for her prompt and professional help and support in publishing *Secrets of Zynpagua: Return of the Princess.*

Thank you God for showering your blessings always.

My faith in Lord Shiva, Gayathri mantra, Shirdi Saibaba and Nam Myo Ho Renge Kyo, has given me the strength and conviction to live my dreams. I know God is there, standing by me in all my decisions.

The little wonders- The voracious Readers of today, tomorrow and forever...

These little kids provide a glimpse of the young population of India who love to read.

Suhasini Seth: born on 30th August, 2001 is a very caring child who loves to read.
This lovely little girl studies in class 7th.

Saanvi Mehra: born on 4th July, 2005. This 9 years old little genius, loves to read, has a personal blog and a library. Much of her leisure time is spent with books and books!

Aarna Malhotra: born on 17th April, 2008. This 6 years old little gadget girl, loves to explore the new technology in her own way. Needless to say, she can operate any gadget. Her fondness for reading through the kindle gives a glimpse of our sharp, tech savy, young population. She inspired me to create the character of Aarna Malhotra in the book.

Viti Mehra: born on 15th April, 2011. This cute, 3 year old is following her sister Saanvi Mehra's footsteps in spending her time in learning to read.

Vanya Sharma: Born on 15th September, 2009, is a fun loving and caring child. She has a great memory, remembers every minute detail of her experiences at various places and interactions with various people. She loves swimming, dancing, painting and reading. She currently resides in California.

Sachinth Goel, born on 12th December 2006. This 7 years old little master studies in Ryan International, Goregaon Mumbai. Loves to read, play cricket, travel and explore the unknown. He inspired me to create the character Sachinth Goel in the book.

Priyanshi Kanhere born on 21st June, 2008. She is very fond of painting and her favourite pastime is reading and listening to stories.

Aadivir Singh (Nickname Adi): born on 7th November, 2009 is Mr. Popular in school, loves to chat, read lots of books and discuss with his daddy. His younger brother is Abhijay Singh, we call him Jay, is born on 4th may 2012. He is a busy bee and loves to go around the house, on his tricycle with his cowboy hat calling eeeh…… haw. They stay in Melbourne, Australia.

Simar: born on 9 th November, 2004 is a wonder kid, fond of reading and playing football. Her younger sister Hiya born on 27th February 2008, is a happy go lucky chirpy girl very fond of dancing and reading.

Fatima Reza born on 11th July 2006, aspires to be a doctor and loves reading, having pancakes and baking. Umairah Hussain born on 14th August 2006, loves dinosaurs and books related to dinosaurs

Arainna Arora, born on 3rd January, 2012, is a charming little baby. She loves to paint and read and play with her friends.

Anhad Singh, born on 29th Jan, 2013. A wonder kid with an adorable smile. His fascination for colourful books and story telling sessions is worth noting.

Aadhya N. Sriram, born on 24th of February, 2008, studies shlokas, does amateur theatre, practices gymnastics, and is learning to play piano and western classical music. This all rounder is in Class 2nd and surely loves to read.

Boski, born on August 17, is four year old little hero who loves to jump and dance, paint, kiss his mom on the arm and read.

The Introductory Song of the Book

This is the story of the Princess of Zynpagua.
This is the story of a cursed land.
When this princess was born,
Her mother tried sending her
To another land,
Then
The cloud hid her in its chest,
The wind stopped its breath,
The Sun covered its rays
To ensure no blemish
Hurts her face.
The winds cried aloud,
'Oh, destiny, be kind to her.
Let luck shine on her.
This infant is too fragile
To cover a million miles.'

The rainbow then lent its hand
To carry this infant to another land.
On three sides was the foaming sea,
And one side land studded with trees.

The little birdie on that tree
Asked, 'Who is she?'
The rainbow then opened its arm
To show a baby embodied with charm.

Weeping, it replied,
'She is the princess of Zynpagua.
She is the princess of Zynpagua.
A cursed place where a devil reigns.
A cursed place where a devil reigns.'

Still weeping, the rainbow continued,
'I am leaving this child
On Indian soil
To save her from the curse's turmoil.'
The little birdie then sang the song,
'Oh, destiny, be kind to her.
Let luck shine on her.
This princess is too fragile
To save her region
From a man so vile.'

The rain then came pouring down
To question rainbow for its frown.
Weeping, the rainbow replied,
'Her mother is tied behind the Moon,
Waiting for her doom.'

The rain then assured,
'Destiny will be kind to her.
Luck will shine on her.
She will grow fast
To rescue her mother
From the curse of the past.'
The rainbow smiled and nodded.
'Oh, yes! Destiny will be kind to her.
Luck will shine on her.
This princess will save her land.'

Yes, destiny will be kind to her.
Luck will shine on her.

(To hear the song and get introduced to the characters, please visit https://www.facebook.com/pages/Secrets-of-Zynpagua-Return-of-the-Princess)

Prologue

That was the dawn of hope rising bravely from the conspiring night. None imagined that it would be *she* who could challenge the time. Yes, no one but Susainna knew as she waited with hope and purpose—her daughter would do it in due time.

She smiled with the memory of the day when the stars had transferred her mystic abilities to her infant daughter and sent her to the Earth. Now she had to patiently wait for her to grow in the safe hands of the Indian family. Her eyes swelled up with tears with the memory of the rainbow leaving her daughter at their doorstep. How the lady of the house had jumped to find the infant girl and had hugged her affectionately. Sussaina's daughter was instantly adopted by the Indian household. They named her Anika.

Sussaina wept and wept. The memory of sending her frail daughter immediately after her birth, ached her soul. But what could she have done? Drudan would have killed her.

Oh, what a beautiful baby she was.

Sussaina silently sat in one corner of the shadowed region and began to murmur the words:

She would rise,
From the coyness of her existence,
To let the world shine with brilliance,
To challenge the stones, the stars, the air, and the clouds,
To clean the muck her people would never be proud,

Yes, my girl will return to question *Drudan* for his crime,
And give back the most beautiful time.

Sussaina began to sing this song, with tears glimmering like pearls on her cheery face. She knew her misery had come to an end. At last, her daughter had found a home and would grow up in no time.

Chapter 1

The Revelation

The chill of the evening was slapping her cheeks. Anika ran ahead while Radhika pursued behind, asking her to stop. Radhika was taken aback by the abrupt change in her little sister's reactions. They had come for the usual evening walk in the woods. Though there was a startling change in the weather, more shocking was the transformation in her sister's response. The gust of wind had hastily befallen with a strange gurgling sound, pushing the pine trees to sway violently and drop cones everywhere. Radhika was surprised how night had suddenly crept in the realm of evening. Anika had panicked with the impulsive change in the climate. The full moon shone with all its might, and the stars stood sprinkled around it. Anika was trembling as she ran, her face utterly impassive and her callow hands trying to clutch her white frock. She opened her mouth and strained her face, but there was no sound. She wanted to cry, but tears refused her. All that she could manage was to gape at the Moon that was walking silently amidst the clouds. After some time, her lips moved slowly, and she yelled, 'The Moon is calling, I have to read the stars!'

Terrified listening to her own voice, she ran.

Radhika dashed behind. The current of air held her back from catching up with her sister. She tried harder to approach Anika but, in the attempt, hit her foot on a pointed boulder, lost balance, and fell crashing on the knees.

She was furious and screamed, 'Anika, what is the matter?'

Her knees and palms were bruised.

She yelled again, 'Anika, stop, I am hurt!'

Anika abruptly halted and turned towards Radhika. She saw the flow of blood from Radhika's knees and palms, her gasping for breath and trying to stand, her flushed face wet with perspiration, yet she remained pale and blank and her legs shook uncontrollably. In a dazed state she continued repeating 'I know I can read the stars!'

With that, Anika fell and lost consciousness.

Radhika dragged herself, trying to reach Anika. While Anika was ten years old, Radhika was also young, only thirteen, but was struggling to maintain a brave front, to control her nerves and forget the acute pain rising from her limbs. She was regretting coming to the woods in the evening.

Before this event, grandma's house had been paradise. Their grandparents were professors in Shillong University, where the two sisters had come to spend their summer vacation. Shillong, a magnificent hill station and the capital of the state of Meghalaya in India, was truly an abode of clouds. The university campus was laden with patches of pine trees. The breathtaking breeze, the descending clouds, the memorable trip to Cherrapunji, everything had been a dream come true, away from school and hectic life in Mumbai, where their parents worked in a multinational company.

Radhika at thirteen was a lovely girl, with long black hair and beautiful brown eyes. The right cheek flaunted a cute dimple that had won many admirers. Despite her popularity, she remained humble and kind, with her attention entirely on Anika. Her younger sister Anika was a coy and quiet girl. She disliked the sight of homework and dominating teachers. She kept her hair short to avoid getting into the puzzle of braiding them. Anika had wheatish Indian complexion and big dark brown eyes. A speck of gold sparkled through these eyes making her look extremely attractive. The innocent charm of her face was veiled by the burden at school. The summer vacation every year in the arms of Shillong rendered a wonderful break, away from the ruthless teachers and demanding homework.

Now things were different. Radhika was panicking. Her sister had fainted in the jungle, and it was already very dark. She knew her grandparents would be back from work and be anxious on not finding them in the house. She somehow crawled and reached Anika. Garnering all her strength, she held Anika's shoulders and tried making her sit, but failed. Engulfed with despair and pain, she began to weep. It was past seven in the evening when Agnis, the helper in the house, finally approached the woods. She shrieked seeing Radhika and Anika lying in the dark. Agnis assisted Radhika to stand and said, 'What happened? I have been searching for you girls for over an hour. This forest is inundated with snakes, and you are lucky to not have encountered one. Your grandfather has gone out to seek the aid of other professors to find the two of you.'

When Agnis saw Radhika had no strength to respond, she said, 'Okay, dear, don't worry, I will fetch someone for help.' She then paused and said, 'It is unsafe here and I do not want to leave the two of you behind. Radhika, I will carry Anika. Will you be able to walk?'

Radhika gathered courage and assisted Agnis in carrying Anika home. Grandmother was stunned seeing Anika unconscious and Radhika bleeding. She immediately called her husband and the doctor.

Radhika kept cursing herself; she was the elder one and should have been more responsible. No one talked till the doctor came. He checked Anika and construed it to be a regular frailty due to excessive bingeing on snacks. He advised some energy drinks and fruits for her. Blood was still oozing out from Radhika's knees, but her entire concern was Anika. The doctor instructed grandfather to bring Radhika to the dispensary for stitches. What an unpleasant evening it had been!

As soon as Radhika and grandfather left for the dispensary, Anika began to toss and turn in the bed.

Grandmother prepared pomegranate juice for her. Seeing Anika's reluctance to drink the juice, Agnis stepped in and said, 'This juice is made from special pomegranates. Your grandfather's friend got them from Spain.'

Anika suddenly sat up in the bed and began to tremble. She murmured, 'Spain? Who is in Spain?'

Grandmother looked perturbed and said, 'Why are you shaking? What happened, darling?'

Anika feebly responded, 'No... Nothing. I am feeling very cold.'

Grandmother covered Anika with two layers of blankets and said, 'I am putting out the lights. You must sleep,' and then left.

The room was dimly illuminated by the night lamp. After some time when Anika opened her eyes to check the time, she saw a young boy standing in the glass of pomegranate juice kept near her bed. She screamed aloud, but her mouth emitted no sound, only her eardrums turned numb. Speechless in terror, she watched the boy come out of the glass, soaked in juice.

He came nearer to Anika and said, '¡Reconocerme!'

Anika was trembling, but when she heard the boy's voice, she felt better. He was speaking in an unknown language. To Anika's surprise, she understood what he said. It meant 'Recognize me!'

Before Anika could say anything, the boy waved his hand and, saying 'Adios amiga vendre otra vez' [Goodbye, friend, I will come another time], jumped in the juice glass and disappeared

Anika cried aloud calling her grandmother. She came in running and, seeing Anika scared stiff, flung her arms around her and said, 'What happened, dear?'

Anika began to weep. She could not tell anyone what was going on. There was neither fear nor anxiety but an excruciating pain of missing someone. She felt her loved ones were crying out for help. This boy seemed to be someone dear and close.

Anika sobbed and sobbed.

She questioned her grandmother, 'Grandma, do I belong to your family? Did my mother give birth to me, or did you pick me from somewhere?'

Aghast, Grandmother said, 'What is the matter with you, Anika? What kind of question is this? Did someone say anything to you?'

Anika began to cry and said, 'Then why do I feel that I have left my family behind. They need me. They are in trouble!'

Grandmother hugged Anika and said, 'Darling, you are missing your parents. Let me call them.'

Anika felt better speaking to her mother in Mumbai. Post the call, grandmother picked the glass of juice and insisted, 'You must finish this.' Anika hesitated. Grandmother forcefully made her drink the entire glass and then switched off the lights and instructed Anika to sleep. Now, alone in the room, Anika felt that her body was melting, floating in the air and heading towards a destination.

After a while she found herself ascending an uneven road. There was snow everywhere. The mighty mountains were capped with white chill and air-puffed ice. With her hair tangled and hands clinging around the chest to avoid the chill, Anika staggered on her feet, swaying a little every now and then. The thin flakes of snow were progressively falling on her, determined to conceal her completely. Anika was silently marching towards the flickering light on the mountaintop. Was it a cave? She could not fathom from a distance. Yet she climbed ahead, her petite tunic and a feeble cardigan contributing insignificantly to save her from the wrath of cold. She knew she was searching, desperately searching for someone. On reaching the mountain peak, she courageously walked towards the light that shone in the adjoining cave. There, beside the fire, was seated the same boy who had appeared in the glass containing pomegranate juice. He was in his early twenties, with blonde hair and fair complexion. He wore a long black coat over a white full-sleeved shirt that had frills at the wrist and neck. His black stockings complimented his black shoes. While Anika stood bewildered, he jumped with a start, delighted to see her. Tears of joy rolled down his eyes.

ANIKA

He started to speak in the same strange language.

'¡Mi espera ha terminado! ¡Usted ha venido!'

Anika could comprehend that he was saying 'My waiting is over! You have come!'

She asked him, 'Who are you?' The boy looked at her blankly. Anika questioned again, now in the same strange language he spoke, '¿Quién eres?'

The boy replied, 'Mi nombre es Federico.' [My name is Frederick.]

Just then Anika was sucked in by the air. The next moment she was back on her bed in Shillong. She faintly heard the voices of her grandma and Radhika. They were calling out her name. Radhika came running inside the room and angrily questioned her, 'Where were you? Why were you not answering when we called your name?'

She then rushed out to inform her grandparents that Anika was in the room. As Radhika left, Anika saw that her sister's knees and hands were bandaged. She felt miserable for causing so much trouble to her family.

She went out and apologized to everyone in the house. 'I am sorry, I was just here.'

Radhika furiously responded, 'Where? We have been searching for you for the past half an hour, but you were nowhere to be seen. Where were you?'

Anika hesitated and then lied, 'I was sleeping beneath the bed.'

Radhika yelled at her, 'Are you crazy? Why are you behaving this way since evening?'

Grandmother stopped Radhika and instructed the two girls, 'Okay, stop fighting and go to sleep. It is eleven in the night. We should sleep now.'

FREDERICK

Anika cuddled beside Radhika and tried sleeping but could not.

She remained distracted and lost in the days that followed. Whenever she looked at the Moon, she felt a lady call out to her. Someone very close, like her mother. When she slept at night, she felt she was walking towards Frederick sitting in the cave, surrounded by snow-capped mountains.

Her dazed state disturbed everyone at home, including her doting sister Radhika. After a great deal of persuasion, Anika told her about Frederick. Radhika did not believe her and told her that she was imagining. Thus Anika stopped confiding even in Radhika.

Frederick had become a regular feature who appeared whenever the pomegranate juice was served to Anika. He stopped speaking though; only his stressed countenance sent butterflies in her stomach. She tried talking to him, but he chose silence until one day when the weather seemed particularly rough and the pine trees outside did a mad dance. That night sleep came easily to everyone except Anika. She crept inside the kitchen and made juice from the pomegranates brought from Spain. Frederick appeared instantly but looked more perturbed than ever before.

He spoke—yes, he did speak this time, '¡Los árboles se balanceaban, y la Luna está llamando! Lea las estrellas!' [The trees are swaying, and the Moon is calling! Read the stars!]

Anika's entire body was shaking, and she murmured, 'I know the trees are swaying, and the Moon is calling, I have to read the stars!'

Frederick disappeared, but Anika continued repeating the lines until dawn.

Anika's grandparents grew very worried seeing her state, and soon the two sisters were sent back to Mumbai in the sweltering heat of summer, despite their summer break still being on.

Back in Mumbai, for almost two weeks, Anika did not see Frederick or hear the call of the Moon. Then one day, Anika's father returned from the office carrying with him a huge box of chocolates.

He called the girls and said, 'Radhika and Anika, come fast. See what I have got for you!'

Both the sisters excitedly opened the chocolate box. Anika lovingly asked her father while biting into the chocolate, 'These taste so different. Papa, from where did you get them?'

Her father responded, 'My friend got them from Spain.'

Anika froze. 'Spain?'

She rushed inside her room and closed the door.

Her father kept calling from outside, 'Anika, what happened?'

Anika replied, 'Nothing, I have a bad stomach.' She stood near the washroom door, staring at the chocolate, fearing to see Frederick.

Sure enough, he jumped out from one of the nuts in the chocolate and said, '¡Hola amiga, su hermano Vivian está llegando a llevarte con él!' [Hello friend, your brother Vivian is coming to take you with him.] And then he disappeared, leaving Anika shocked.

She had begun to believe that all that transpired in Shillong was indeed a figment of her imagination until Frederick resurfaced. She remained restless the entire day and could not get any sleep in the night. When everyone else had slept, she went to the kitchen to have water. The kitchen had a glass window, which faced the sky. As she drank water, she noticed the sky. It was a new moon night, and there were no stars. All of a sudden she heard a buzzing sound. She strained her ears trying to locate the bee that was emitting the sound. To her dismay, she realized that it wasn't a bee but a voice coming from the firmament.

The voice said, 'Anika, my daughter, come fast, your mother is tired! Come fast!'

Anika was so frightened that she began to weep. She ran to the bedroom and covered her face with a blanket and howled.

Her life had changed, and no one was ready to believe that!

Chapter 2

Vivian

It was pouring outside, but the rain did little to assuage Anika's mood. The reappearance of Frederick and the familiar painful voice from the Moon contributed in tarnishing her frame of mind. Anika's father was very worried seeing her state and made her join theatre classes.

On the first day of the class, the hall of the theatre was inundated with students chirping excitedly for their newfound hobby. Miss Annie, the play director, walked in smiling. Her small pretty face flushed colour as the heels of her pointed red shoes made the knock sound. She welcomed everyone and then introduced the play to the children. It was called the *Return of the Thief.* Radhika was selected for the main lead to be the queen while Anika was to play a cameo role as the confidant of the thief. Everyone spent a week rehearsing the play which was to be showcased on the coming Saturday.

Days went by and with them took away Anika's wretched state. She loved the practice sessions. Saturday came fast, bringing with it the excitement of presenting the play. The girls hurriedly dressed up. Anika's one eye was darkened with black colour to give her the guise of a thief while Radhika looked stunning as the queen. Miss Annie introduced the play to the audience and then called Radhika to start the first act. Anika was nervously peeping from the backstage, waiting for her turn.

On the stage, the thief had entered the queen's room, and it was now Anika's turn to make an entry. She confidently announced her arrival, went running on the stage, and delivered a humorous speech. The audience laughed and cheered. Anika continued excitedly but, after a while, forgot the lines and began to mumble. The prompter yelled from behind, but Anika could not remember her lines.

At that moment, a young boy leapt from the roof of the stage and made a dramatic entry. He delivered an outstanding speech and saved the play. Before he left, he carried Anika on his shoulders and waved farewell to the audience. The play proceeded successfully. Anika was very relieved to see him and said, 'Thank you so much! Who are you? Did Miss Annie send you?'

The boy smiled and said, 'Anika, my sister, I am Vivian!'

Anika turned cold. The colour from her face faded, and fresh drops of perspiration appeared. She murmured, 'Vivian?'

The boy pleasantly sat beside Anika and placed his hand on her shoulder. He said, 'Dear sister, please don't be afraid of me. I am your brother from Zynpagua.'

VIVIAN

Anika was shaking with terror.

Seeing Anika's state, Vivian spoke in a melodious voice that appeared to be coming from a far-off land, 'Dear Anika, recognize my voice. We have been waiting for you for ten years. Hear me, my dear sister! Don't be frightened, I have come to take you to the place you belong.'

And then he sang a song.

My dear sister, you have come,
To undo the crime that was done,
Our mother is lost in the shadow of the Moon,
The clouds are crying and calling you soon,
You promised her you will come,
You have come, you have come!
Now please be brave and show us the way,
The stars will protect you till the last day,
Read their signs and find the path,
Now keep your promise and undo the crime,
Please give us back the most beautiful time.

The song put Anika in a state of trance; her soul
was floating in another world. Shadows of the
past kept flashing back in her memory.

Seeing her state, Vivian said, 'Anika, I will tell you everything. Don't worry, please don't worry. I can tell you everything, but not here, in our world.'

Anika murmured, 'In your world?'

Vivian hesitated and then replied, 'Yes, in Zynpagua.'

'What? Zhyn... pagua? Which place is this? I have never heard of it,' asked Anika.

Vivian smiled. 'No one has heard of this place because it is cursed. It was a part of the Earth that got separated from it.'

Anika still could not believe Vivian and said, 'No, there is no place as Zynpagua.'

Vivian said, 'Yes, Zynpagua exists, and you have to come there!'

Before Anika could say anything, Vivian looked towards the western direction and hastily said, 'I have to go now. Anika, I do exist. It's not your dream. You are my sweet sister. Please come with me to my world. See you soon,' and he disappeared.

Radhika came in hurriedly from the door on the west and hugged Anika. 'Wow! The play is a hit. We have been asked to repeat it next Saturday. You were exceedingly humorous. Who was that boy?'

Anika distractedly muttered, 'My brother.'

Radhika was taken aback and asked, 'What?' Then looking at Anika's state, she chose to change the topic. Their parents joined them as well, and everyone headed towards the exit. Even they were curious to know about the blonde boy who dramatically carried Anika from the stage. Anika remained silent.

While sitting in the car, Radhika whispered, 'Anika, are you all right? Is it the dream of Frederick or something else?'

Anika simply replied, 'Nothing. I am fine.'

When they reached home, Anika cuddled beside Radhika and slept.

After some time, a crashing noise woke her up. It was the sound of the windowpanes hitting the wall. Outside, the clouds rumbled and the breeze raged. Anika walked towards the window to close it, but the wind blew harder and a splash of rain entered the room and drenched her. She pulled out a towel to wipe herself, but a voice alerted her, 'Wait!'

She looked down and saw Vivian dancing on a drop of water. He regained his height and hugged Anika. To Anika's surprise, she was not scared of him now; instead, she hugged him dearly. On looking at Vivian closely, she realized that he resembled her. He had the same set of dark brown eyes with a speck of gold in them. The difference was in their complexion and hair colour. Anika's complexion was a shade of brown and she had black hair while Vivian was very fair and had neatly cropped blonde hair. He looked very handsome in a pair of denim jeans and a crisp white shirt.

Anika smiled at him and asked, 'Dear brother, how old are you?'

Vivian smiled and said. 'I am fifteen. I have been waiting for you since the last ten years.'

Anika was aghast. 'For ten years?'

Vivian responded, 'Yes, for ten years. Dear Anika, please come with me to Zynpagua. I will tell you everything.'

Anika objected to his request, 'My family is here. I can't leave them.'

Vivian responded, 'Dear sister, thirty minutes in your world are equal to thirty days in Zynpagua. Please come for thirty minutes, no one will know. I will ensure they sleep till you are back.'

Anika questioned yet again, 'How will you ensure that they sleep till I am back?'

Vivian smiled. 'Through magic.'

Anika was shocked. 'You know magic? How?'

Vivian promised that he would tell Anika everything once they are in Zynpagua, but Anika insisted.

Vivian then narrated the story.

'Zynpagua was once a region on the Earth. It was ruled by King Soto and Queen Sussaina. Queen Sussaina was a very kind and intelligent woman.

'One day she noticed that the stars send signals to the Earth. These signals were like a pre-warning before any calamity. Sussaina tried reading the stars and, after years of trying, began to identify their signals. Gradually she began to predict the future by recognizing the indications sent by planets and stars. She judiciously used this skill to protect the people of Zynpagua against any calamity.

'The planets and stars were deeply impressed by her deeds. They blessed Sussaina with the ability to influence them. Each planet could send its benefic rays for good causes. Thus Sussaina became the only woman who had the power to ask planets to send their virtuous rays.

'Once there was a drought in Zynpagua. Due to lack of rain, the crops did not grow. There was no food to eat and the people were miserable. The farmers were in a wretched state. Sussaina tested her virtue for the first time and prayed to the Sun for help. Listening to her prayer, the Sun sent its benefic rays and inundated the fields with magical crops. A single grain could fill the stomach for the entire day. Whoever consumed these grains became healthy and strong. People from other regions specially came to Zynpagua to buy these crops. The farmers of Zynpagua became prosperous.

'After some days, Sussaina read the stars and found that the king of a neighbouring kingdom was silently coming to attack Zynpagua. His army was triple in strength to that of Zynpagua, and his soldiers were coming on horses, elephants, and tigers. Sussaina alerted King Soto, but there was very little time to prepare for war.

Sussaina then prayed to Mars to grant valour and courage to her soldiers. Mars sent its benefic rays, and the soldiers of Zynpagua became valorous and strong. They defeated the enemy in seconds. Zynpagua then earned the reputation of having the best army on the Earth.

'When the farmers of Zynpagua became the richest and the soldiers became the most valorous, people from around the world wanted to get their daughters married to these farmers and soldiers. The farmers and soldiers started acting pricey and asked for unnecessary favours to marry anyone's daughter. Unfortunately, Zynpagua became a male-dominated society. This angered Sussaina. She prayed to Venus to grant the women of Zynpagua valour, beauty, intelligence, and education. Venus sent its benefic rays and made the girls of Zynpagua ravishing beauties endowed with intelligence and valour. These girls were proficient in horse-riding, sword fighting, farming, mining, and mathematics. Through their intelligence and mathematical acumen, they became the best trade planners. People started consulting them for various trades and business. King Soto hired them for training new soldiers. Kings from far-off lands started coming to Zynpagua requesting these gifted and beautiful women to marry them. Thus the girls of Zynpagua became world famous for their special abilities.

'Sussaina had made Zynpagua a gifted land. She prayed to the stars to help her people and did not ask anything for herself.

'King Soto and Queen Sussaina had no children. Queen Sussaina treated her husband's younger brother Frederick as her own son. He was eight years old. One day Frederick went to the forest with his friends but did not return. The king's soldiers searched every nook and corner of Zynpagua but could not find him. The queen was devastated. Seeing her sorrow, the stars blessed her with a son, Vivian. The king and queen were elated by the birth of their son. For the next five years, their attention was entirely on Vivian, and they forgot to take care of their kingdom. Due to their neglect, evil and malice began to spread in Zynpagua.

'There lived a crooked scientist in Zynpagua called Drudan. He realized that the king and queen were neglecting their kingdom. He joined King Soto's palace as a minister and secretly began to plan king's assassination. He relentlessly worked in the laboratory to create an electronic weapon that could kill King Soto. After five years of trying, he invented a violet light that could spread like wind and annihilate anyone. But Drudan knew Sussaina would be able to save her people by impressing the stars. Thus he wanted to learn magic to become invincible.

'In these five years, Drudan also pretended to be concerned about the welfare of the kingdom and became king Soto's favourite minister. The king and the queen treated him like a family member.

'Queen Sussaina had a friend named Pajaro, the princess of clouds. She was human in form, could fly like birds, and was blessed with magical qualities. Drudan wanted to learn magic from her and began to impress her. Pajaro fell in love with him and married him. They were soon blessed with a son, Leo. He inherited the qualities of his mother. Drudan's powers began to deplete whenever he faced Leo. He despised his son and wanted to kill him.

'Pajaro then taught magic to Drudan to pacify him and save her son, Leo. As soon as Drudan learnt magic, he combined his scientific research and magic and invoked the fatal violet light. The violet light spread like lightning over Zynpagua. It was so charged that even Drudan could not control it. The violet light began to generate catastrophic movements in Zynpagua. Soon these movements became so violent that they separated Zynpagua from the Earth. It vanished in the universe, carrying with it all the people on that land.

'This infuriated the planets. They blamed Sussaina and Soto for neglecting their kingdom. It was due to their negligence that Drudan had become powerful and his wicked intentions had brought so much suffering. The stars took away their blessings from Sussaina as a punishment for neglecting her kingdom.

'King Soto tried saving Zynpagua, but the violet light hit him and he got sucked in the universe. Drudan captured Queen Sussaina by deceit and locked her in the shadow behind the Moon with an evil spell. The shadow behind the Moon is the darkest area in the universe where the evil spells can work best. Sussaina tried influencing the stars and rescuing herself but could not do so.

'Drudan's vicious act infuriated the Sun and the stars, and they refused to send their rays to Zynpagua. This separation cost Zynpagua heavily, and it stopped receiving the sunlight. It became the cursed planet. Pajaro could not save Sussaina but hid Vivian. Drudan searched for Vivian everywhere and, on not finding him, hit Pajaro and wounded her. He took his four-year-old son, Leo, with him. Pajaro was fatally injured and could not follow Drudan to save Leo. Before she died, she kissed Vivian on his forehead, thereby transferring her magical powers to him. She also cast a protective spell on a mountain range and hid Vivian there. Thus Vivian was saved from Drudan, but Pajaro died.

'While Queen Sussaina was imprisoned in the shadow of the Moon, she realized that she was pregnant. She knew if Drudan discovered this fact, he would kill her child in the womb. She prayed to the stars to save this child. The stars felt pity on Sussaina but told her that they had to abide by the law of the universe which states that every human being has to pay for his deeds. By neglecting Zynpagua, Sussaina and Soto had invited evil and had brought disaster for Zynpagua. Therefore, Sussaina and Soto would have to pay for their deeds.

'However, the stars picked the child from Sussaina's womb. It was a baby girl. They asked the rainbow to carry this child to the Earth. The stars then told Sussaina that they had granted this baby girl with the power to influence them. One day their baby girl will hear the call of nature and come back to save Zynpagua.'

Vivian's voice was choked by the time he finished narrating the story.

Anika was stunned to know about Zynpagua. She asked Vivian, 'Dear Vivian, how can I help you?'

Vivian smiled and tears rolled down his eyes. He said, 'Anika, you are the fragile infant who travelled from Zynpagua to the Earth. I am Vivian, the son of King Soto and Queen Sussaina, and you are my sister.'

Anika gasped. 'What?' She was trembling and could not say a word. After a while she said, 'Vivian, I think you are mistaken. I am not your sister, and I have no special powers!'

'Yes, Anika, you are my sister, and you have inherited the powers. It is you who can read the stars and influence them. Dear sister, we need you to rescue our mother, to free Zynpagua from the clutches of wicked Drudan.'

'How do you know that influencing the stars will bring an end to Drudan's rule?' asked Anika.

'Because... I can hear Mother Sussaina's voice. She told me to bring you back from the Earth. Only you can influence the planets to cast their benefic rays and end Drudan's rule,' Vivian answered sadly.

Anika thought for a while. She had been hearing a painful voice coming from the Moon. She asked Vivian, 'But when the planets are seeing that Drudan is cruel, why can they not send their benefic rays and end Drudan's rule?'

Vivian smiled. 'Because, dear sister, our parents neglected their kingdom and brought misery for their people. Only their children can fight the nature's curse and free them and their kingdom!'

Anika was left with no option. Her heart was telling her that Vivian was not lying. She asked Vivian, 'How will we go?'

He replied, 'With the whirling wind.'

Vivian looked in the north-west direction and raised his hand to call the wind.

Anika intervened, 'How will the wind come? It is raining.'

Vivian smiled. 'Look!'

Anika could see a cyclonic dust storm come towards them. Soon they were swirling with the wind. She grabbed Vivian's hand firmly and felt the rotating wind engulf her. Within minutes they were racing in the sky with the force of the wind. Anika could vaguely see huge boulders hanging in mid-air, her vision diminishing with every swirl, and sensed her skin turn cold as they soared higher and higher. They were steadily approaching a huge black oval-shaped structure. When they were very close, Anika yelled in pain. She felt her eardrums tear with the air pressure and she fainted.

When she woke up, she found herself amidst a celebration.

Chapter 3

Zynpagua

The crowd was cheering aloud as they watched the chariots, driven by bullocks, race with each other. The bullocks were fiercely charging towards the destination. The man on the red chariot overtook the one on the yellow, and the gathering burst out enthusiastically. Anika noticed that all the riders had worn black stockings and a blue jacket. She guessed that it could be the uniform for the race. Only the man riding the yellow chariot had also worn a white turban that covered his hair and face. The racing chariots were blowing the dust that the mighty breeze carried with it everywhere. The milieu was flooded with the encouraging uproar of the men and the thundering sound of the drums signalling a celebration. The crowd was full of sickly looking men with shrivelled skin and rugged sinews.

Anika whispered to Vivian, 'Where are we?'

'In Zynpagua,' said he.

Anika noticed that the entire place was lit by huge lamps. She asked Vivian, 'Is it night-time?'

Vivian sadly replied, 'No, it is daytime. We have not seen the Sun since our mother was captured. Look at the sky.'

Anika looked up and was aghast to see a dark black sheet without any stars, only a faint feeble Moon and smoky clouds speckled around it. 'Oh my god!' She sighed.

Vivian replied, 'Yes, life without the sunlight is terrible. People of Zynpagua have become weak and are ailing.'

The beating of the drums brought Anika's attention back to the race.

'What are the people celebrating?' asked Anika.

'Today is the Annual Chariot Race Festival. Drudan will reward the winner. While the commoners are occupied in watching the race, you change your guise here before anyone notices,' Vivian replied.

Vivian peeped straight in Anika's eyes and murmured, 'Change and exchange.'

Her pink frock transformed into a silver tunic. A black band appeared in her cropped hair, and her shoes were replaced by sturdy brown boots. She was fascinated by her new look. Anika remembered something and immediately checked her pockets. A smile flashed on her face to find the Spanish chocolate which she had carried with her.

Vivian looked at the chocolate and enquired, 'What is this?'

Anika sheepishly replied, 'This is the Spanish chocolate.'

Vivian's attention went back on the race that was taking place.

Anika checked her dress and a question popped out in her mind. She asked Vivian, 'How did you change my dress?'

'By magic,' Vivian replied smiling. Seeing Anika's bewildered look, he continued, 'Lady Pajaro, wife of Drudan, gifted me with magical powers before she died. They are equal and opposite to those of Drudan. He can use his magic only for doing evil, and I can use mine only for the good of others—' Before Vivian could complete, a huge hullabaloo diverted his attention. When the two turned, the man with the white turban had won the race. The trumpets were being blown signalling the arrival of King Drudan. Two black horses came charging in, mounted by fierce-looking warriors. They pushed the throng to the sides, clearing the pathway. Then a group of children came in running and sprinkled red flowers on the road. Two men walked in, blowing the trumpets. Anika noticed that the crowd suddenly became silent as they looked up in the sky. She was about to scream at the sight, but Vivian covered her mouth. A huge bee was descending from the sky. As it came closer, Anika saw a ferocious-looking man, wearing a crimson gown on his lean body, sitting on the bee. Vivian whispered in her ears, 'That is Drudan, bow your head.'

Anika saw that the people had bowed their heads as Drudan dismounted the bee.

A boisterous laughter echoed and frightened everyone. Anika slightly raised her head and strained her eyes to see Drudan. He was a tall man with dark sunken eyes. His skin was shining unusually as if he had painted his face with silver. His dirty brown hair was braided, and a violet light was circling around it. There was an eerie calmness in his expressions. He walked towards the podium and slapped a minister. It was such a tight slap that the minister's cheek turned blue. Drudan came closer to him and said, 'How dare you look at me in my eyes!'

The minister fell on his knees and said, 'I am sorry, my lord.'

Drudan kicked him and walked ahead. Pulling out a bottle from his pocket, he announced, 'Who is the winner? Come and take your reward!'

No one stepped forward. He laughed aloud and said, 'My people, this is the sweetest poison I have ever made. It tastes like honey and kills in seconds. Come, swallow it.' No one moved.

Anika whispered in Vivian's ears, 'Why is he offering poison?'

Vivian alerted Anika, 'Shhhh, don't talk. He is a crazy man.'

Drudan inspected his surroundings. Everyone had bowed his head and was trembling.

Satisfied, he turned to the minister who had been slapped. 'Drink it!' he said, smiling maliciously.

The minister was shaking with fear. Tears rolled down his eyes, and he said, 'Pardon me, my lord.'

Drudan's face stiffened, and he repeated, 'Drink it.'

The minister quietly took the bottle from Drudan and gulped the poison. The crowd shook in fright. When he had finished having the poison, a thick golden chain appeared in his neck.

Drudan laughed aloud and patted the minister. 'Fool, you are alive. I have given you a golden chain as a gift for obeying me.'

The minister was still trembling and fell on Drudan's feet. 'Thank you, my lord.'

Drudan laughed aloud and said, 'Thank Friday. I don't kill anyone on a Friday.' He then turned to the crowd and said, 'You have wasted enough time. The winners come forward immediately. I have better things to do.'

As the winner approached closer, his white turban fell off. A gorgeous-looking girl with long black hair was standing there, instead of the man.

FEMINA

Vivian gasped and said, 'Oh my god! This is the fisherman's daughter Femina.'

Drudan fumed and said, 'You wicked woman. How dare you come out and compete with men. I will kill you!' Then a thought made him smile, and he said, 'No, I will give you a punishment worse than death. You will rust in my jail. Soldiers, arrest her.'

The soldiers arrested Femina.

Vivian cried aloud, 'No!'

Someone from the mob slapped him. Another pulled Anika by the hand and took her with him.

Drudan was announcing in his thunderous voice, 'This lady Femina has the audacity to take part in a game meant only for men. Such impudence by any woman has never been tolerated. She has challenged our moral system. Women are meant to be behind the four walls of their houses. Put her behind the bars. I am going for a visit to the seven kingdoms. Once I am back, I shall decide her fate!'

The assembly cheered, and then one soldier dragged Anika to the king.

Drudan bellowed, 'Who are you?'

Vivian hurriedly came forward and pleaded, 'My lord, this is Anika, my sister. I am a poor farmer, my lord. We were simply passing by. Please grant forgiveness, my lord.'

The king ordered one soldier to slap Vivian and Anika. It was such a hard blow that cut Anika's lips, and she began to bleed. Vivian fell on the ground.

When the king had left, Anika stood up, crying, 'Why did you not use magic on him?'

Vivian seemed very disturbed, yet he controlled his anger and said, 'Because Drudan is more powerful. We cannot revolt against him till we can fight his powers. That violet light around Drudan's hair can kill anyone instantly. Drudan captured mother with this violet light.'

Anika thought 'the violet light was like an open electric wire from which sparks were emitting. It was indeed a fatal weapon'

Anika whispered in Vivian's ears, 'Drudan does not recognize you?'

Vivian said, 'No, because Pajaro's magic protects me.'

'Why can women not participate in any games?' asked Anika in a low tone

Vivian replied softly, 'That is because Zynpagua is known to give birth to miraculous women with extraordinary powers. Drudan fears one of them will bring his death.'

Anika feebly asked, 'How will we fight such a powerful man?'

Vivian unintentionally responded, 'Only the Sun and the stars can help us fight Drudan. Anika, you are blessed with the power to influence the planets. We can save Mother with their help!'

Anika stared at Vivian and asked, 'Do you know Frederick?'

Vivian instantly asked her, 'How do you know Frederick? He was our uncle who disappeared.'

Anika was perturbed. 'Frederick was our uncle? Oh yes! You told me our uncle disappeared when he was eight years old. I know him. He is in a place covered with snow and speaks a different language, which I am able to understand. In fact, I travelled there after drinking the pomegranate juice. He resurfaced from a Spanish chocolate recently and said, "The Moon is calling. Read the stars!" He also informed me that you were coming to take me!'

Vivian jumped with joy. 'Our uncle is alive? He knows me? How did he know that I was coming to meet you?'

53

Anika responded, 'I don't know, dear brother. Next time when I meet him, I will ask him everything.'

Vivian was silent for some time and then said, 'I have been living alone for the last ten years! I know how difficult it is. Is our uncle also alone?'

Anika thought for a while and said, 'I think so, but I am not sure.'

Vivian asked yet again, 'But why can he not come to Zynpagua when he could come and meet you?'

Anika sadly replied, 'Dear brother, I do not know anything. I have carried the Spanish chocolate. On swallowing it, I will reach the place he is in. I can then ask him about everything.'

Vivian was in tears. 'I have found my sister and my uncle. One day we will rescue our mother as well.'

He voiced aloud,

'A day will come
When the Moon will be milky white.
The Sun, Venus, and Mars will be ready to fight
To destroy the shadow
And rescue our mother.
You can do it, no other.
Impress Sun, Venus, and Mars.
They are eager to use their powers.
Our freedom lies in the hands of stars.
They will shower their blessings like flowers'.

Anika repeated the line, 'Impress Venus, Sun, and Mars?'

Vivian nodded and said, 'Yes, sister, Mother told me that by impressing the Sun, Venus, and Mars, you would bring an end to Drudan's rule in Zynpagua.'

Anika looked at Vivian and said, 'Does mother Sussaina speak to you?'

'Yes. I can hear her voice sometimes.'said Vivian

He noticed blood trickling from Anika's lips and plucked a leaf from a nearby plant and applied it on her bleeding lips. The flow of blood stopped immediately.

Anika questioned Vivian yet again, 'How are the trees and plants growing here without the rays of the Sun?'

Vivian replied, 'The trees and the plants loved our mother. They refused to leave Zynpagua with the Sun when she was captured. The Sun cannot let any innocent being die and therefore promised them to send invisible rays to form chlorophyll.'

'Oh! I see,' said Anika.

Vivian suggested, 'Anika, let us go home.'

Anika gratefully nodded and followed Vivian. A peasant was passing on a bullock cart, and Vivian requested him for a ride. He readily agreed.

'There are no cars here?' asked Anika

Vivian laughed. 'Cars? Dear sister, Zynpagua is a cursed land, primitive and dying. People here have become weak and fragile without the sunrays. They are unable to use their mind to develop technology. They can only ride bullock carts here. If we are not able to impress the Sun, life on Zynpagua will fail to exist!'

Anika was horrified by this revelation. 'How will I impress Sun, Venus, and Mars?' She thought

Vivian's voice got her back from her reverie. He was saying 'We are now passing through the residences'

As the cart moved ahead, Anika saw little houses built of wood and mud with walls of reed stuffed with straw. These petite brown structures were symmetrically arranged along the uneven road.

Houses in Zynpagua*

She also saw simpletons sitting in a group. Few men had their chest bare that flaunted a scorpion tattoo. Their bodies were lean and bony with shrivelled skin. Some wore stockings while the others were wearing ill-fitting pants. On moving ahead, Anika saw a group of men with turbans, preoccupied in weaving a cloth; few others were peeping from a shop-like structure, set amidst the array of houses, selling metal artefacts. Everyone looked ill and famished.

'I cannot see any women here!' said Anika.

'They stay indoors,' replied Vivian.

'Do women look as weak and famished as these men?' asked Anika

'No, because they have been blessed by Venus' replied Vivian

Anika thought, *Femina was indeed a gorgeous-looking girl. Were all the girls of Zynpagua as pretty as her?*

The cart hurriedly crossed the houses and reached the foothills.

Anika and Vivian got down and thanked the man. Hunger kicked Anika's stomach, but she maintained silence and ascended the mountain. When they were at the hilltop, Vivian pointed towards a huge house made of brick with thatched roof that flaunted a creeper blooming with red flowers. It was the most appealing, and peaceful place which cajoled Anika to run inside and sleep in its arms. She dashed towards the door and opened it. There was a living room and a tiny kitchen towards one corner of the house and a small room towards the other end.

Fatigue had taken its toll on Anika, and she looked pooped. Vivian rushed to cook something for her. He lit the clay stove stacked with wooden twigs and made the most delicious porridge Anika had ever tasted. While having the porridge, Anika noticed that Vivian was looking very disturbed.

Vivian's house*

Anika asked him, 'Why are you so upset?'

Vivian replied, 'I am worried about Femina. God knows what punishment would be given to her.'

'Do you know Femina?' asked Anika.

He nodded his head and said, 'Yes. She is my friend. One of the most learned, brave, and intelligent girls in Zynpagua. She excels in horse-riding, best at fighting with bows and arrows, swords, and poles. King Drudan is a vicious man. Under his heinous rule, people have become cowards. I wish I could kill Drudan.' Vivian was livid with fury.

Anika inquisitively asked him, 'How old is she?'

Vivian was controlling his temper. In a low voice he said, 'She is seventeen, two years older to me.'

Seeing Vivian's expressions, Anika murmured, 'We have to save Femina!'

Vivian seemed to like Anika's suggestion as his countenance relaxed and he said, 'Anika, we will think about this tomorrow. You are very tired, please take some rest.'

He placed two cots woven with coir outside his house for them to sleep. Anika lay on the cot and tried sleeping. She was so tired that she did not even remove her boots. The memory of Femina and Drudan's ferocious face continued to nag her.

She then thought of Frederick. He was her uncle who had disappeared from Zynpagua. Frederick had informed her about Vivian. Anika decided to approach him for a solution to save Femina. She pulled out the Spanish chocolate from her pocket and popped it in her mouth.

The air began to suck her in until her legs hit something hard and wet. Her sturdy boots dug deep in ice on the frozen mountain. The icy breeze was forcing Anika to bend backwards as she continued her ascent. Her tunic fluttered with the roaring zephyr, and she turned blue in the cold.

Shivering, she yelled, 'Frederick, ¿dónde estás?' [Frederick, where are you?]

There was no sign of Frederick. Her voice echoed and vanished. Anika tried locating Frederick beyond the river, near the sheer-sided gorges, above the stony slopes, between snowy summits, but could not find him. As she stepped further on the snowy surface, a sinking feeling engulfed her. She felt the sensation of a heartbeat beneath the snow, and her legs vibrated with every beat. Before she could bend and place her ears on the ice, Frederick came skating from behind one of the slopes. He aggressively waved at Anika. Hola, Anika! ¿Cómo estás? Bienvenido a nuestro mundo.' [Hi, Anika! How are you? Welcome to our world.]

Anika repeated, '¿Dónde estoy?' [Where am I?]

He responded while removing his skates and the woollen cap that covered his blonde hair, 'Esto es Siepra Nevada, montaña cerca de España. Esta es una región invisible.' [This is Siepra Nevada, mountain near Spain. This is an invisible region.]

Anika asked Frederick '¿Hablas en qué idioma?' [You speak in which language?]

Frederick responded 'En español el que he aprendido de las personas en las inmediaciones region.' [In Spanish, which I learnt from the people in nearby region.]

He smiled and continued 'Todavía cometo errores al hablar español' [I still make mistakes while speaking Spanish]

Anika laughed and said 'Creo que incluso cometer errores mientras habla español' [I think even I make mistakes while speaking Spanish]

After sometimes, Anika blurted out the question that was nagging her, 'Tú eres mi tío. ¿Por qué desapareciste de Zynpagua?' [You are my uncle. Why did you disappear from Zynpagua?]

Frederick's countenance stiffened. He coldly replied, 'Querida Anika, te diré un día, ahora no.' [Dear Anika, I will tell you one day, not now.]

Anika got nervous seeing his angry face.

Seeing Anika, Frederick smiled and said, 'Gracias a Dios que has llegado Zynpagua. Mira la estrella brillante en el cielo. Ve ahora, usted está congelando aquí. ¡Adiós! [Thank God you have reached Zynpagua. Look at the bright star in the sky. Go now, you are freezing here. Goodbye!]

Anika felt someone pull her back on the bed. She could not understand why Frederick was incensed. She was sad as none of her questions could get an answer. Tired and helpless, she silently closed her eyes and tried sleeping.

After some time, a sound distracted her. She gathered her senses and tried focusing on the sound. It was Sussaina's voice. Anika felt motherly affection all around her, and she turned numb. Gaining her senses, she tried hearing what the sound was saying. Her eyes swelled up as she heard Sussaina weeping. Her mother was saying, 'My darling daughter, you have come, you have come...'

Anika murmured, 'My dear mother, don't worry. I have come, I have come. I will save you, my lovely mother. But please help me. How can I impress the Sun, Mars, and Venus?'

Sussaina's voice whispered, 'By your virtues, my darling. Find someone's true love and Venus will be delighted.'

Anika murmured, 'Find whose true love, dear mother?'

But Sussaina could not respond. Instead, Anika heard Sussaina crying out in pain. Images began to flash in front of her eyes. She saw her mother, fragile and wrinkled, tied in chains and a violet light gyrating around her body.

Drudan, ugly Drudan was standing beside her and saying, 'Violet, engulf her, give her so much pain that even her soul cries out. She transferred her powers to her daughter. Now let her die. She called her daughter to Zynpagua. How dare she?' Then he spoke aloud, 'Wait, Violet, wait. Let me give her real pain. Let me bring her daughter's dead body in front of her eyes.'

Drudan laughed and said, 'Yes, real pain… her daughter's dead body!'

Sussaina howled and said, 'No, Drudan, don't touch my daughter!'

Drudan mercilessly laughed. 'Yes, I will… How dare you hide your daughter from me. I will kill her.'

The images vanished suddenly. Anika was crying profusely. Her body ached like never before, and she felt the pain would split her. After some time, the pain subsided, but she continued to cry. She went running to Vivian and narrated the entire episode to him.

He replied in disbelief, 'How does Drudan know that you have come to Zynpagua?'

'I don't know how.' said Anika

Vivian took a deep breath and said, 'The violet rays must have informed him about your advent. Damn!'

Anika was trembling as she said, 'I could see Drudan torture Mother!'

Vivian sighed and said, 'I know, Anika. Sometimes, Mother tries connecting with me, but the image of Drudan torturing her starts flashing in front of my eyes. Mother breaks the connection just then so that Drudan is not able to reach us. My sister, I have been seeing Mother's miserable state for years but am unable to do anything.'

Anika howled and hugged Vivian, 'Brother, we will save her, you don't worry!' she said.

They wept till sleep replaced sorrow in their eyes. When Anika woke up, the firmament was still a clear black sheet ornamented with a feebly visible Moon. As Anika continued to ogle at it, she saw a spark in the sky, in close proximity to the Moon. It was a star and soon it began to sparkle. Anika was astounded as she felt the strength of her body flowing up, trying to reach the sparkling star. Powerlessly she continued to gape at the sky and gradually went off to sleep.

Next morning, when she woke up, she was bustling with energy. She rushed inside the house searching for Vivian. He was cleaning a sword and turned to respond but, on seeing her, stood up with a start 'Anika, your face is shining! What happened?' he asked.

Anika told Vivian about the sparkling star.

'Dear sister, it is a miracle that you saw a star. None of us have seen stars for years. This is very encouraging! Anika, what was in your mind before you went to sleep?' asked Vivian.

'I was thinking of a way to save Femina.' Anika said.

Vivian voiced excitedly, 'Then maybe the appearance of this star is linked to saving Femina!'

Their conversation was obstructed by the sound of thundering drums coming from the fields below. Vivian ran towards the sound, and Anika followed, sprinting down the hill to the fields. The drummer was announcing,

Loyal men of the King,
Be ready to sing,
In the wedding ceremony of Femina,
With our old farmer Dohrna,
The event will happen three days from now,
The king will donate a cow,
Let us rejoice and dance,
For her brilliant chance,
Loyal men of king,
Go dance and sing!

The simpletons were blindly applauding and praising the king. They bellowed, 'Long live our kind kings!'

Vivian got furious listening to the announcement.

'Is Femina getting married to an old man?' asked Anika

He replied, 'Yes, he is ninety years old sick man. Look there.'

Anika saw an old man wearing a garland made of marigold flower, sitting quietly in a cart that was a part of the procession. His aged skin was moulded and his sunken eyes were lost deep in thought.

Anika exclaimed, 'Is he Dohrna?'

Vivian replied, 'Yes, that is Dohrna. He is old and ailing. Even his grandchildren are married now. The king is ruthless. It is all a big game for him. Anika, we have to do something!'

Anika replied, 'I know, brother, but what can we do?'

Vivian angrily replied, 'Break into the prison and save Femina?'

'How will we do that? We don't have any weapons' asked Anika.

'My dear sister, saving a woman from meeting a miserable fate is a virtuous task. I can use magic for virtuous deeds. We can both go and save Femina' replied Vivian.

Anika and Vivian went home. Vivian had been very disturbed and spent the day sharpening his sword and some other weapons, while Anika kept thinking of how to impress the stars. She prayed to God to help her learn the ability to read the signs sent by stars. She looked towards the sky. It continued to be a dark sheet. There was no trace of sunlight. Anika joined her hands and called out to the Sun. There was no sign of encouragement from any corner. Exasperated, she covered her face and kept thinking- when she could not see any star, how would she read their signals? The thought of saving Femina was haunting her. She kept trying till her head began to hurt. Tired and depressed, she sat down on the cot but her heart continued to call out, 'Save Mother! Save Femina! Save Zynpagua!'

As she touched her forehead, she realized it had become warm. She assumed it was due to the headache and went and drank water. Then she came back and sat on the cot. She felt a prickly feeling on her forehead again and, on looking up, noticed a ray of light coming from the horizon, literally tearing the sky with its sharp bright beam.

She could not believe her eyes and continued to gape at the sky. Overwhelmed with surprise, Anika ran to call Vivian. Pointing at the sky, she asked Vivian, 'Can you see that?'

Vivian looked up and asked, 'What?'

'The sunray' said Anika, excitedly.

Vivian looked up again and tried hard to find the ray. Disappointed, he said, 'Sister, I can't see any ray.'

Anika looked up to show him the ray, but could not see it. 'I saw the ray' she murmured

Vivian smiled and said, 'Dear sister, I think you are stressed. You should relax.'

'Yes, brother, I think I am dreaming. I can't read the stars!' said Anika, sounding dejected.

Vivian noticed that Anika was looking very sad and tried reassuring her, 'Dear sister, it is a divine gift bestowed on you. Try connecting with nature, the sky, the earth, the air. You will surely be able to get the answers.'

Anika spent the rest of the day trying to observe the various elements of nature. Whenever she thought of Femina, she felt some warmth on her forehead. On looking up she could see the single ray of Sun again and then it would disappear. This continued to happen the entire day. Anika realized that the appearance of the slanting ray of the Sun was connected with the thought of saving Femina.

She tried linking the various elements of nature with the thought of rescuing Femina. She murmured,

'The sunray came thrice,
The star too winked twice,
The Moon was dimly white,
Then why should Femina have to fight,
For her destiny's right?
The stars are indicating marriage to royalty,
A man bestowed with ability,
To end this era's crime,
And rule this region in his prime.'

She called out to Vivian. "I can read the stars! I know I can read the stars! Femina is destined to marry a royalty, a king. I can see it. A handsome man endowed with chivalry and valour.'

Vivian voiced angrily, 'How?'

Anika said, 'I know this is going to be the future but don't know how. We have to rescue Femina from the prison. The Sun is sending signals, wanting me to rescue Femina. This is all connected. Vivian, we have to do something.'

The two made a plan and commenced walking towards the prison. The jail was in a tall fort with walls made of strong bronze pillars and huge boulders cemented with mud and clay. The roof of the fort had a double-layered balcony studded with attentive militia. Each end of the fort had an enormous circular stand on which fire was lit that illuminated the entire area. The entrance of the fort was a robust gate made of bronze and copper which was guarded by eight soldiers.

Anika darted towards them. One of the soldiers caught her by the hand and questioned her.

'How dare you come here?'

Anika boldly replied, 'I have come to rescue Femina.'

The soldier laughed and wedged her. Vivian immediately made an eye contact with the soldier to hypnotize him. He said, 'Sleep like a snake and do not wake.'

The soldier fell on the ground and curled up like a snake. Anika marched ahead with Vivian rallying behind, raising his hand and spellbinding everyone to sleep. Unfortunately, one of the soldiers, who hid from Vivian's gaze, drummed the bronze plate. This served as a warning alarm for all the soldiers, and they came in running towards the entrance and the convict's cell. Anika could not pace with Vivian and fell rolling down on the slide that elevated to the prisoners confinement.

Two armed men came from behind and hit Anika on the head. She fell on the floor, began to bleed and fainted. This enraged Vivian, and he ran towards the soldier and jumped on his chest. He then drew the dagger from the soldier's belt and pierced it straight in his stomach. Pulling the dagger out, he turned towards the other and ripped his neck. He then picked Anika and carried her on his shoulders towards convict's cell.

On approaching the cell, Vivian saw that Femina was tied in metal chains, with her face swollen and blue with bruises. Vivian was shaking with rage and hit a blow at the cell door. Exasperated, he backed out as the door did not break. He lifted his hand, but the magic did not work. He knew anger was an evil emotion, and his magic would not work for anything evil. He placed unconscious Anika on the floor and searched for something to break the lock.

Femina's eyes swelled up with tears on seeing Vivian. She gratefully cried out, 'Thank you, Vivian, Thank you so much!'

Vivian was desperately searching for something to break the lock.

Femina cried out, 'Use your magic.'

Vivian replied, 'I can't!'

They heard footsteps of the army marching towards the cell. Vivian tried waking Anika but she did not get up. In a state of desperation, he shook her hard. She woke up with a start.

Vivian cried out, 'Dear sister, please brace courage, I will carry you back but help me now, I am unable to do magic.'

With a splitting headache and blood smeared on her shirt, Anika dragged herself towards the cell door. After thinking for a solution, she put her little finger in the keyhole of the lock and grimaced in pain. Vivian tried pulling her finger out, but it had got stuck in the keyhole.

Anika winced in pain and pleaded, 'Brother, please break the lock with magic.'

Vivian lifted his hand again and, looking at the lock, said, 'Open!'

This time it worked and split the lock into two. Femina was tied to a metal chain circled around her. As Anika advanced forward, trickles of blood oozed out from her forehead, and she dropped, writhing in pain.

Femina warned Vivian, 'I can hear the agitated voices. Hurry up!'

Vivian tried helping Anika to stand and said, 'We cannot go out. I will have to call the wind. Anika, please tie yourself with Femina!'

Anika courageously stood up and, with the help of Vivian, wriggled and got inside the circle of metal chain that tied Femina.

She gasped for breath and said, 'Brother, please hasten, I can't breathe, and the chain is splitting my skin.'

Vivian panicked when he saw blood oozing from Anika's head and hands. The chain was splitting her skin. He lifted his hand and said, 'Winds of north and south, take us out!'

The breeze blew and a storm could be seen coming towards them. Soon they were swirling with the wind.

Chapter 4

True Love

Femina burst into tears on reaching Vivian's house. She was grateful that Vivian had saved her but was worried about her father's safety. Vivian left Anika and Femina at home and went to bring Femina's father- the fisherman. When he reached his house, he saw Drudan's soldiers whipping the fisherman. He fought with the soldiers and wounded them. Then he brought the fisherman home. The fisherman was bleeding and unconscious. Femina nursed him, and when he came back to consciousness, he was shaking with pain and fright. He continued to repeat that Drudan would kill him and Femina and it was better that they commit suicide.

Anika was standing outside the door and was very disturbed seeing the scene. She asked Vivian, 'Brother, how will we bring an end to Drudan's rule?'

Vivian too looked despondent and said, 'Dear sister, you have the power to influence the stars. You will gradually learn to use this strength of yours. Our mother is also with us. She is guiding us whenever possible. Pajaro has gifted me with magical abilities which will save us from Drudan's vicious spells. It will take time, but we will rescue Zynpagua and our mother from the clutches of Drudan.'

Vivian's assurance did build some confidence in Anika. Her stressed countenance relaxed. After a while, she politely questioned Vivian, 'Dear brother, if you are confident that I would read the symbols sent by stars correctly, then why did you get so angry when I told you about Femina's future?'

Before Vivian could answer, a cool and refreshing breeze broke their attention. The milieu was overflowing with heavenly fragrance. The clouds burst into a drizzle and the parched ground rejoiced and emitted an earthen tang that cajoled everything around to dance. The trees gracefully relented and swayed merrily with the wind to demonstrate their obedience.

Anika noticed a silver line descend from the clouds and transform into an elderly woman. She came closer and said, 'Dear children, I am Lady Carol and have descended from the kingdom of clouds.'

Vivian and Anika were taken aback and could not respond.

When Lady Carol did not receive a response from them, she continued, 'My daughter Pajaro was married to evil Drudan.'

'You are Lady Pajaro's mother?' Vivian immediately spoke out.

'Yes. Pajaro was my daughter who married Drudan against our will. Evil Drudan murdered her!' said Lady Carol, her eyes swelling with tears. Sobbing, she continued, 'I have been searching for my grandson Leo, the son of Drudan and Pajaro. He is special and is destined to rule the kingdom of clouds. In fact, when my grandson was born, Drudan's powers began to deplete. Drudan detested Leo and has hidden him somewhere. I have been getting nightmares and feel that his life is in danger. Vivian, I know that Anika has returned to Zynpagua. I have come to help you kids and to find my grandson.'

Anika had been silently observing Lady Carol. She asked her, 'Where is the kingdom of clouds?'

'Kingdom of clouds lies beyond the Moon. It is the abode of humans who can fly and are gifted with magical powers. We live on clouds, and our sky is inundated with blooming roses, making the kingdom of clouds the most beautiful and pristine place in the air. Birds of seven shades reside in these roses, and when they fly, the sky gets painted with rainbow colours. None of us ever ventured out from our world except my daughter Pajaro. Her curiosity to discover the world beyond the Moon made her reach Zynpagua. It was the most flourishing and technologically advanced region of the Earth. There, she met Sussaina, and they became friends instantly,' Lady Carol told Anika. Memories of the past lit her sad face for a while as she continued, 'I loved my daughter. She was a very gifted girl and would have ruled the kingdom of clouds. Drudan tricked her into marrying him.' Saying this, she began weeping profusely.

Anika comforted her and, in order to draw her attention away from her sorrow, asked, 'How did you know that I have arrived?'

Lady Carol replied, wiping her tears, 'Anika, my darling, when Pajaro died, I tried rescuing Sussaina and told her to influence the stars and free herself. Sussaina then informed me that the stars had transferred her powers to her daughter and sent her to the Earth. She requested me to take care of Vivian. I have been following Vivian for years but did not come close, fearing Drudan might harm him. Zynpagua can only be rescued if the Sun and planets decide to send their beneficent rays. Anika, my darling, only you have the power to influence the stars. I have been waiting for you and have descended to be your guide.'

Anika's head began to throb. So many people had been waiting for her to save them. Zynpagua was her kingdom, and she had inherited the power to save it. The question, 'how to influence the stars?', nagged her even more.

Lady Carol inquisitively asked Anika, 'Darling, are you able to read the symbols sent by the stars?'

Anika hesitated and said, 'Yes... after trying for hours I have been able to decipher that Femina will marry a king.'

Something made Vivian very angry, and he snapped at Anika, 'How are you so sure? Who is this king?'

Anika and Lady Carol were taken aback by his terse response. Vivian immediately realized his mistake and apologized.

Lady Carol asked Anika, 'What makes him so upset?'

'I don't know. Did I say anything wrong?' asked Anika.

Lady Carol smiled and said, 'Of course not. We will soon find out why Vivian is so upset.'

Anika continued, 'Vivian has been tense since the time Femina was arrested but now she is free. I really do not know why he looks so upset. I may have made a mistake in reading the stars.'

Lady Carol encouragingly replied, 'Anika, while reading stars requires practice and dedication, it is the person's intuition that shows the way. Your inner voice has told you about Femina's future. It cannot be wrong. Remember, my child, once you are able to read the signals sent by stars, you can slowly start impressing them. Winning their favour is the only solution to Zynpagua's miseries. You have made a steady progress. Don't be disheartened, sweetheart!'

She looked up at the sky and said, 'Anika, I will go now but will join you tomorrow. The kingdom of clouds has no ruler, and I am worried that my absence would encourage some alien invasion. I will make arrangements for the safety of my people and return soon. In the meanwhile, do not forget to learn sword fighting and horse-riding from Femina. You have to be well equipped to face Drudan.'

Anika hugged her and said, 'Goodbye, grandma!'

Lady Carol hugged her back and soon she could be seen flying in the sky till her image blurred in the horizon.

Vivian silently waved at Lady Carol and then lay on his cot, pretending to sleep. Anika had been extremely tired. She intended to speak to Vivian, but sleep took control of her and she dozed off.

Anika was in deep sleep when someone called out her name. With eyes half open, she saw Femina standing near her cot, trying to wake her up.

'Good morning, Anika. Did you sleep well? Vivian informed me that I have to teach you horse-riding and sword fighting. When can we start?' asked Femina enthusiastically.

Anika got up half-heartedly and requested Femina to give her some time to freshen up. She came back soon and energetically announced, 'I am ready!'

Femina had a sword in her hand, and on seeing Anika, she threw it in her direction and said, 'Catch it.'

Anika missed the target and the sword fell on her feet. She yelled in pain. Femina ran towards her and said, 'I am sorry, but fighting with the sword is all about agility. The quick movement of limbs ensures a win, otherwise defeat is certain.'

Anika apologized and requested Femina for another try.

Femina picked the sword and threw it towards Anika. The shining metal of the sword blurred Anika's vision, and she missed her target again. This time, the sword fell on the ground.

Femina gently smiled at Anika and said, 'Don't worry, this happens to everyone. We will continue trying till you are perfect.'

She repeated the act ten times till Anika could jump like lightning and hold the sword. Then Femina picked her sword and began training Anika. It required a great deal of focus. Anika's fragile hands could barely manage to hold the lethal weapon. In no time, she looked drained and pooped. Femina continued the training, pushing Anika to exert with every attempt. Gradually, Anika began to control her moves. Once Femina was satisfied, she announced, 'I guess this is enough for the morning!'

Anika was grateful. Her hand was hurting and her head throbbing. Vivian had prepared breakfast and called everyone for the meal. Femina left to take bath while Anika filled her plate and hungrily finished the breakfast. After eating, she asked Vivian, 'Where is the washroom? I want to bathe.'

Vivian smiled and said, 'Dear sister, we do not have washrooms in Zynpagua. We bathe in the river. Femina has gone there. Go follow her.'

He pointed towards a brook flowing down the hill.

Anika saw a thin little rivulet surrounded by huge trees, which made the place very secluded and hidden. She ran down the slope towards the water body and saw Femina coming out after bathing. She looked stunning with long black hair, pink complexion, big black eyes, and an elegant gait. Anika thought, *She deserves to be a queen one day.*

On seeing Anika, Femina steadily walked towards her and asked, 'Is your hand still hurting?'

Anika smiled and shook her head. 'No, I am fine,' she said.

Femina patted her shoulders and began to ascend the mountain. As Anika turned to wave goodbye to her, she saw Vivian hiding behind the tree, with his gaze fixed on Femina. This was the first time Anika grasped that her brother was deeply fascinated by Femina's charm. With this realization came the worry that Femina would be married to a king. Anika kept thinking about Vivian's unreciprocated love while bathing. Who would this king be? This question continued to echo in her head.

She understood the reason for Vivian's ill temper. 'He knows he cannot marry Femina!' she murmured.

She finished bathing and went back to the house thinking about Vivian.

After sometime, Femina commenced teaching Anika and Vivian how to use metallic thunderbolt, daggers, armed spears, and bow and arrows. Vivian kept snapping at Femina. She reacted incredulously and said, 'What is the matter? Why can you not focus? When you taught me horse riding, I obediently followed you. You are being the most obstinate today!'

Vivian threw the dagger which was in his hand and walked away.

'He taught you horse-riding?' asked Anika.

Femina was livid and said, 'Yes, he did. He is the best in horse-riding and sword fighting. I think his talent has got into his head. Look at the way he is reacting.'

'I will speak to him. I feel there is something bothering him miserably,' said Anika and requested Femina to leave her alone with Vivian for some time.

Femina went inside the house.

Anika kept thinking on how to bring up the topic. She decided to question Vivian directly and asked, 'You are in love with Femina, aren't you?'

Vivian was knocked for six. The colour from his face faded, and he looked even more upset. When Anika repeated the question, he tetchily divulged, 'Yes, I love her. But what is the point? She is destined to marry a king. I have liked her since childhood, always thought she would be my soulmate...'

Saying this, Vivian hit his fist on a nearby rock. When Anika tried comforting him, he said, 'We are not destined to have a normal life, my dear sister. With mother locked in the shadow of the Moon and father untraceable, I cannot even think of leading a normal life. God only knows what the future has in store for us.'

Anika wanted to cry herself. She hugged Vivian and while holding him, said, 'Dear brother, everything will be fine, and all of us will lead a normal, happy life.'

Vivian did not react. After sometime, he asked her, 'Can you do me a favour? Please find out who Femina is destined to marry. I will kill that man. I cannot live without her.'

Anika got perturbed seeing Vivian's reactions. She said, 'Dear brother, I am still learning how to read the stars! Why are you taking my prediction so seriously? I could have made a mistake.'

'No, it is not a slip-up. The tone of your voice was not habitual when you said that. It had the affirmation of future events!" responded Vivian, sad and dejected.

Anika was shocked to hear that. Had she actually begun predicting the future? Which power was pushing her to construe the signals sent by the stars? Was she really receiving some clues from nature? How could she be so confident in predicting Femina's destiny?

'What happened, dear sister?' asked Vivian, observing Anika's stressed face.

She tried camouflaging her feelings and said, 'Nothing.'

Vivian patted her and said, 'I have given you enough trouble. Dear sister, I will handle it. Don't get worked up because of me.'

Before Anika could answer, Vivian walked away, still lost in his thoughts.

When Vivian had left, Anika vigorously shook her head to let go of any unwanted thoughts. Getting her focus on whom Femina would marry, she began concentrating on the question. She looked around to find clues from the environment.

Vivian's state venomously discomposed her. She looked up at the dark sky to see if there were any stars. But alas! The firmament was a dark sheet with no trace of the stars. It was daytime, and even the Moon was absconding. Anika spent the day trying to find a sign but failed.

The advent of the Moon in the sky gestured the arrival of evening. Fatigue and worry made her head spin. She got up and went looking for Vivian. As she headed towards the house, a chuckle diverted her attention.

Femina was trying to teach Vivian how to use a thunderbolt, and to Anika's relief, they were laughing. A ray of light was transcending the clouds and reaching Vivian's forehead. It gave the look of the setting Sun. Anika was shocked to see the ray. She rubbed her eyes to be sure that she was not daydreaming. Yes, it was a ray. Anika called out, 'Vivian, can you see the ray?'

Vivian looked up and said, 'Which ray? I cannot see any ray!'

Anika pointed towards the sky but the ray had disappeared. Vivian saw her expression and said "You are tired. Take some rest'.

Anika nodded and went and sat on a chair in the balcony. She did not want to disturb Vivian and Femina. Her head was spinning with the memory of the transcending ray. She murmured, 'the setting Sun signified the end of a life.'

Appalled, Anika began to focus. Just then a fierce gust of wind blew from the east, carrying with it some loose leaves from the tree. Anika turned and looked towards Vivian. Two such leaves and a flower got stuck in Vivian's hair. Anika was petrified. What was nature trying to indicate, and why were all these signs connected with Vivian?

Her heart was beating fast. She began to shake, and tears rolled down her eyes. What was happening to her? Femina noticed her from a distance and came running towards her.

'Are you all right Anika, why are you shivering?'

Anika immediately stood up and tried covering up. 'There is a nip in the air. I am feeling cold.'

Femina laughed. 'Cold? In this warm season? I think it is time to start our practice again. You need some action. Let me teach you how to use the bow and arrow.'

Anika silently undertook the bow and arrow training in the evening, but the symbols continued to bother her. Femina was very impressed by Anika's performance and subtly teased Vivian, 'Anika is better than you. Mr Distracted Stubborn Man.' Vivian shot a rude glance at Femina. She blew air in his ears and ran.

Anika thought, *Is Femina also in love with Vivian?*

Femina's father came out limping. He was feeling better and insisted on going back to his house. Femina tried opposing, but he was relentless. Vivian agreed to drop them off the coming day.

Anika was watching them from the balcony. She thought *was nature trying to indicate danger to Vivian's life when he would go with*

Femina and her father? Fear made her shake and sent tremors in her veins. What was destiny trying to indicate?

At that moment, they heard the beating of drums. The sound was coming from the foothills. Vivian instructed everyone to be indoors while he went to check the reason of the commotion. Anika insisted on going with him but he sternly denied.

Vivian did not return for more than two hours. Anika felt that nature was sending a message of threat. She continued to regret having sent Vivian alone. After a while, Femina announced that she was going to look for Vivian. Anika resisted the idea as she knew it was not safe. Just then, they heard the galloping of a horse. As it approached nearer, Anika saw Vivian slumped on the horse with his forehead bleeding. They shrieked aloud and dashed towards him. Vivian was unconscious. Anika and Femina made Vivian dismount the horse and lie on the cot. He lay there for almost an hour, murmuring incoherently. Anika tried waking him, but Femina stopped her. She bandaged his head with cloth and some herbal leaves and let him rest.

When Vivian came back to consciousness, he informed them about the commotion. Old farmer Dohrna, whom Femina had to marry, died. The king had ordered the soldiers to search for Femina and Vivian. One of the local people recognized Vivian and informed the soldiers who attacked him. Vivian pulled a soldier from his horse and mounted it. He fought with the rest until someone hit him on his head. He somehow managed to escape on the horse.

Vivian told them that Drudan had come to know about Anika's advent. He had declared a war against Vivian, Femina, and Anika. He had announced that anyone who supported them was an enemy of the kingdom and would meet his death.

After listening to Vivian, Anika was very tense and nervous. How could the three of them stand against entire Zynpagua?

When the others had gone to sleep, Anika quietly recollected the events of the day. She continued to contemplate the meaning of the signs. She murmured

'The Moon replaces the setting Sun in the night,
The withered leaves fall, and the fresh ones arrive,
Cool breeze blows and reduces the summers plight,
Change is inevitable, and the world continues to fight,
To find the best who can achieve great height,
Before dusk fades, it indicates the direction
Who shall be the next in succession?
The rays fell straight on Vivian's head,
The three leaves and a flower showed a crown instead,
Vivian will be the king, who will save the world from disgrace,
Justice and compassion will he embrace,
And the centuries will praise his race.'

Anika repeated the lines.

'Oh yes,
Vivian will be the king, who will save the world from disgrace,
Justice and compassion will he embrace,
And the centuries will praise his race.'

Anika danced with delight. 'My brother will be the king who will save Zynpagua from disgrace. He will be the king whom Femina would marry. Oh yes! This is all connected.'

Anika's head began to hurt again. She felt the same sinking feeling in her heart.

Her instinct kept telling her that these symbols were also signifying an end. An eerie feeling told her that these signs had a double meaning; Vivian to be the future king of Zynpagua but also signalled the end of a sibling of the king. She was the only sibling Vivian had. Was she deducing the end of her own life? She quietly murmured.

'But beneath this hope lies a dying soul,
The king's kin whose life had a goal,
The violet light she could not escape
Death came in a murky drape.'

Was it death that was coming her way? She was euphoric discovering Vivian's future but perplexed about her own. She glared at the sky and noticed that it was a full moon night. The Moon appeared the brightest that night. She sat beneath the dark sky, motionless, trying to predict her own future.

Her thoughts were broken by thunder and lightning. She looked up and saw fireworks in the sky. Terrified, she ran to call Vivian, but he was not around. Anika looked up again and stood awestruck. A star was sparkling in the sky from which a thick beam was being emitted, directed towards the Moon. It seemed the heavens were shaking. The beam continued to grow thicker, sending its light to the Moon.

Suddenly, the clouds burst, emitting a violet storm. The violet storm took the form of a cyclone and came charging towards Anika. Aghast, she tried running, but the storm began circling around her, stopping her legs from moving ahead. Anika felt dizzy, and her vision began to blur. She could faintly hear a voice call out to her. She strained her eyes to focus on whose voice it was and saw Vivian.

He had mounted a horse and was speedily riding towards her. He was yelling, 'Anika, run, come fast. This weather signifies arrival of the deadly violet light.'

Anika tried to run, but the engulfing wind did not allow her to step forward. Instead, she fell on her knees. As she looked up, she saw a violet shadow enveloping the milieu. It was actively camouflaging the entire area, including Vivian and Anika and their brick house. Another gust of whirling wind came charging towards Anika and swallowed her in it. Her head spun, and she felt the air tear her hands and feet. She wailed in pain. Vivian rushed towards the whirlpool, but lightning stuck him straight on the chest, and he flew back, falling from the horse.

A woman cried out from somewhere, 'Leave my children alone. Please don't harm them!' The voice was cut by a raucous laughter.

Anika felt suffocated in the whirlpool. Vivian got up and tried stopping the wind through magic but was blown away. Both Anika and Vivian could hear the loud weeping sound coming from the clouds.

Just then, the voice that was guffawing cried out in pain, 'No!'

The beam being emitted from the star changed its direction and came straight down, aiming at the violet shadow that was engulfing the region. The wind slackened its grip on Anika, and she fell flat on the ground. Vivian rolled on the ground and reached her. He called for Femina, but she was frantically knocking at the door from inside the house. Someone had locked her in with her father.

SUSSAINA

Vivian was left with no strength to stand up and lift Anika. He lifted his hand in the attempt to cast a protective spell, but was stopped by the sight of a lady gradually descending the beam. When the woman landed, Vivian exclaimed, 'Mother Sussaina!' Tears of happiness flooded his eyes.

The woman was also weeping and just sat there, decrepit and fragile, unable to walk. Lines of sorrow and weariness showed on her face which was robbed of all hope. Her eyes were shrunk by the prominent wrinkles and the dark circles beneath them. Years of torture were distinctly visible on her face. She stretched her hands towards Vivian and Anika and said, 'My children!' and fainted.

Vivian garnered his strength and stood up. He dashed towards Sussaina and held her. He aimed his hand towards the house and murmured a spell to open the door. As the door opened, Femina rushed out and was shocked to see the scene.

Vivian whispered 'Mother!' in Sussaina's ears. She woke up and feebly placed her hand on Vivian's head. 'My Son!'

Femina had sprinkled water on Anika's face and she came back to consciousness. Pointing towards Sussaina, Femina told Anika, 'Mother Sussaina is here. Look there.'

As she looked at her mother, a piercing pain emitted from the depths of her heart. Anika staggered and stood up and dashed towards Sussaina. She hugged her mother dearly and wept and wept. The pain within was tearing her soul into pieces. She held Sussaina near her chest and pleaded, with tears of agony rolling down her eyes, 'Oh, God! Please end this misery. Look at our mother!' Vivian too held his mother and cried aloud. The three had come together for the first time. No one spoke, only their sobs revealed their sorrow within.

Femina hurriedly brought water for Sussaina and made her drink it. Sussaina softly smiled at Femina, Vivian and Anika and hugged them. Vivian asked her, 'Mother, it is a miracle! How could you escape Drudan's evil spell?'

Sussaina was coughing as she answered, pointing her finger towards the sky, 'Look at that bright shining star. It is Venus and is very happy with you, dear Anika. You have been able to discover true love and unite two noble souls who will rule Zynpagua one day. You have impressed Venus, and that is why it sent its full beam on the shadow of the Moon, thereby breaking the vice spells with which Drudan had tied me. Anika, my daughter, I am glad that you have won the favour of one star. Venus is very kind and will now support you. Drudan tried capturing you today, but Venus directed its beam on the violet light and saved you.'

Anika was surprised and asked Sussaina, 'Mother, how I impressed Venus?'

Sussaina smiled. 'You have been able to discover love between two true lovers.'

Before Anika could ask further, Sussaina warned her. 'Dear daughter, while you have impressed Venus, Drudan has come to know about it. This news has made him even more vicious and evil. He will try and harm you, Anika. It is very important that you impress the other stars soon.'

Anika nervously asked Sussaina, 'Dear Mother, I don't even know how I impressed Venus, then how am I going to influence the other stars?'

Sussaina hugged Anika and said, 'Dear daughter, be brave. You helped Vivian rescue Femina. You have been able to predict the future that Vivian will honour Femina's true love and would be the next king of Zynpagua. This has impressed Venus.'

Both Femina and Vivian were overjoyed to hear their future. Vivian hugged Anika dearly and said, 'Thank you, dear sister.'

Sussaina patted Vivian and continued, 'Dear son, the coming time would be tougher than you have ever imagined. My children, I don't want to alarm you, but now you will face a life full of challenges. We cannot deny that Drudan's greatest mission is to end Anika's life. Femina, my child, you are a great warrior. Please ensure Anika gets trained to protect herself!'

Femina bowed before Sussaina. 'I will, Mother. I will teach her and protect her.'

Sussaina called Femina closer and said, 'You are a valiant girl. I am glad that you will be my son's partner for life.'

Femina was weeping as she said, 'Mother. I knew God will answer my prayers. I always wanted him to be my husband!'

Vivian looked at her, absolutely surprised. Femina blushed, and Vivian passed a mischievous smile to Femina.

Sussaina continued, 'Dear son, our struggles are camouflaging this good news. We have to protect each other and fight for the freedom of Zynpagua.'

'Mother, if you will be with us, we can win any battle!' assured Vivian.

Sussaina sighed in grief. 'Son, Venus could rescue me only for a night. Come morning, Venus will lose its powers, and then Drudan will throw me back in the Moon's shadow. The violet light engulfing the milieu was sent by Drudan. He has scientifically created it, and no one knows how to fight it. I am grateful that Venus could save us.'

Vivian could not believe what he heard. 'No, Mother, we will not let you go!'

Anika too cried aloud, 'Mother, you cannot go!'

Sussaina hugged her dearly and said, 'You are my saviour, Anika, and you have come. I am very sure, my dear daughter, that one day you will rescue me from Drudan's clutches.'

Weeping, she continued, 'The pain stayed with me for years when I sent you to the Earth. I have been watching you from behind the Moon and calling out for you. Dear daughter, you have impressed Venus, now you have to impress Sun and Mars. The day you are able to influence them, they will send their beam on the shadow of the Moon and rescue me forever.'

Turning towards Vivian, Sussaina said, 'Vivian, my son, you are destined to be the future king of Zynpagua. Win people of Zynpagua to your side. Eradicate fear from their heart and make them fearless. It is going to be very difficult, but I know you can do it!'

Vivian and Anika sat with their mother for hours till the birds began to chirp, signalling the arrival of morning. Venus began to fade. Sussaina looked up at the sky and declared, 'Now, my children, please go inside the house and lock it. Drudan can arrive any moment. He wants to put me back in the shadow of the Moon. Anika, my child, run inside. Vivian, my son, use magic and create a white glow. Drudan will not be able to cross it.'

Vivian declared, 'Mother, we will save you!'

Sussaina insisted, 'No, Vivian, Venus weakens by morning and cannot support us any more.'

Sussaina's pupil dilated on seeing a violet radiance penetrating the clouds. She shrieked, 'Vivian, hurry, my child, create the white halo, otherwise Drudan will capture Anika!'

Vivian murmured a spell and created a white halo that separated Sussaina from the rest of them. Soon the environs were inundated by loud yelping laughter and the dusty wind. Femina pulled Anika back in the house. The violet beam came speedily, knocking Sussaina and sucking her back in the sky.

Vivian yelled, 'No, Mother!' but the dusty storm filled his eyes with mud, and in no time Sussaina was gone and the wind ceased. Vivian lay on the ground sobbing. Femina came running from inside and called for Vivian, 'Anika is unconscious and is not getting up!'

Chapter 5

Drudan

Drudan winced in pain as he wiped the blood oozing out from his forehead. Raising his hands, he roared, 'Victory is mine!' Then he narrowed his sunken red eyes to check the expression of his ministers. They were trembling and feebly voiced, 'Long live our king!'

Drudan sprang up angrily, exposing his lean and scaly body on which a white gown stained with blood, hung loosely. He menacingly howled 'Only long live?'

With the speed of lightning he rushed towards a minister and held his collar, then dragging him on the floor, came back to his throne and sat again, placing his right leg on the bleeding head. The minister cried aloud, 'Victory and long life to our kind king!'

DRUDAN

The minister shivered and said, 'Mercy, my king!'

Drudan dug his dirty long nails into the minister's face and clawed his skin. Then with his right leg, he kicked the minister and threw him away. 'I am happy today and mercy is granted!' he yelled.

The minister began to weep and joining his hands said, 'Thank you, my lord!' He was lucky to have escaped the death which the queen had faced.

Drudan had slit the throat of his elder queen to activate the violet light. Her head had rolled towards the right on which Drudan mercilessly put his foot. What a gruesome act it had been. With the same sword, he had made a cross on his forehead which signified that the violet light had been sent to do its task. Blood was still trickling out from the cross.

The violet light was Drudan's fatal weapon which he developed with his scientific acumen and evil magic. It inflicted the worst possible death anyone could imagine by entering the veins and blocking the blood supply. This violet light could only be activated by fresh blood. Drudan created it scientifically, but eventually, he made it stronger with his evil magic. Anything evil requires vice for supporting it. Thus Violet demanded fresh blood for doing its task.

Drudan killed anyone whom the violet light wanted to swallow. The light would circle around the person, and Drudan would instantly kill him. People lived in morbid fear, wondering who would be Violet's next target. This time the violet light circled around the elder queen. She was Drudan's favourite. When Violet circled around the queen, Drudan instantly slit her throat, without even a speck of remorse.

In fact he had laughed. 'Violet, you and I share a similar liking. Take her!'

The violet light had swallowed queen's blood and had left the palace to accomplish its task. Drudan could fall to any level to finish his enemies.

Now, Drudan and the ministers were waiting for Violet to return. It had been almost four hours since Violet had left to do its task. Drudan had been getting images of what had been transpiring, and had become more violent with every passing hour.

Suddenly, there was lightning outside. The window burst open and a flickering violet light could be seen returning to the palace. Like a storm, the light spread in the hall. The ministers panicked and felt their energy sap as they desperately gasped for breath. Violet had sucked the oxygen from the air and made it difficult for anyone to breathe.

The ministers knew Drudan had created a chemical which he swallowed every day, to tolerate the presence of violet rays. Thus it was only Drudan who could stand Violet's presence; the others felt choked.

Drudan noticed this effect of Violet on them. He laughed and said, 'Okay, let us play a game. We will call it who will live and who will die. Violet will be around for ten minutes. Let me see who can survive its presence.'

The ministers were shaking. Lack of oxygen made them dizzy. They began perspiring profusely. Soon their faces turned colourless, and gradually they started falling from their seats. Drudan was continuously laughing. One of the ministers prayed aloud, 'My lord, save us. We are your warriors and have supported you against Sussaina.'

The mention of Sussaina distracted Drudan. He called aloud, 'Violet, where is Sussaina?'

Violet light began to flicker and circle around Drudan. He laughed. 'Good, Violet, you have captured her again. Good. Let me go and meet her! Come with me, Violet!'

He then opened his mouth and swallowed the violet rays. With every gulp, his body vibrated aggressively. His face turned blue with pain. He closed his eyes and sat still, with his body shuddering.

After some time, Drudan opened his eyes and laughed aloud. 'Victory is mine! My violet has killed that tiny worm.'

When Drudan had swallowed Violet, the ministers could breathe again. They gasped for breath and feebly sat back in their chair. Drudan looked at them and said, 'My ministers are so weak, and they call themselves my warriors. I think I don't need you. Today, I am happy. Violet has killed that insect Anika. I am going to have a word with Sussaina. Let me share this good news with her. In the meanwhile, you can live for another day.' He walked ahead, and the ministers felt relieved. When he was about to reach the doorway, he instantly turned and said, 'Who is laughing?'

The ministers looked grim. Drudan smiled. 'Good. I hate to see people laugh in my kingdom. Only I have a right to laugh. No one else!' He dilated the pupils of his dirty red eyes and shot a menacing look at them.

When Drudan had left, one of the ministers asked his colleague, 'How can Drudan communicate with the violet rays? I can't hear a word.'

The other minister whispered slowly, 'The violet rays speak to Drudan in higher frequency. Human ears are incapable of listening to such sounds, only Drudan can. He is a scientist.'

'Why do you know so much about me?' asked a voice coming from the doorway.

The ministers instantly turned and saw Drudan standing there. He looked displeased and said, 'My god! My ministers know how I communicate with Violet. Then they must die!'

Before the minister could say anything, Drudan raised his hand and, pointing his fingers towards the two ministers; he pronounced a spell 'Die!'

The two ministers collapsed, and Drudan walked out, leaving everyone else stunned.

Coming outside, Drudan pulled his crimson handkerchief from the pocket and blew air on it. He inhaled deeply and said, 'Fly with me, my crimson bee.' The handkerchief changed into a big bee, and Drudan sat on it and flew, rising higher and higher in the dark sky towards the Moon. As the distance between him and the Moon diminished, a milky glow could be seen. As the illumination grew, Drudan covered his face instantly. No matter how powerful he may be, he knew he could not face the Moon and the stars. They always inflicted some wound on him. As he came nearer to the Moon, he howled in pain. The right side of his face turned silver and wrinkled. He screamed aloud when his right cheek began to throb and swell and instructed the bee, 'Fly fast, my bee, I cannot face the light of the Moon. Reach its shadow as soon as you can!'

This happened every time Drudan dared to cross the Moon and reach its shadow, where he had imprisoned Sussaina. The first time Drudan tried crossing the Moon, his right eye lost vision. It took him almost a year to regain his sight.

Drudan knew Sussaina worshipped the Moon, and the only place he could capture her was the Moon's shadow where the moonlight did not reach. This was where the Moon turned powerless. Though he managed to capture Sussaina through his evil spells and violet rays, he himself dreaded crossing the Moon and reaching its shadow.

Now, when Drudan was going to meet Sussaina, he was not only scared of the Moon but also Sussaina. He knew she was a supernatural lady and the universe favoured her. While the Moon and stars were angry with her for neglecting her kingdom, they would not allow any harm to come to her. Thus despite torturing Sussaina for years, he could not harm her in any way. But today was different.

Today Drudan could hurt her soul. He had killed her daughter Anika—Sussaina's only hope of impressing the stars and saving Zynpagua. He rejoiced in the moment. Violet had entered straight in Anika's heart and annihilated her soul. Anika did not even get the time to transfer her powers to anyone.

Drudan contentedly smiled. 'If no one can influence the stars, then no one can rescue Zynpagua from me. How long can Sussaina survive?'

Another thought entered his evil mind. *If no one will influence the stars, people of Zynpagua will decay and die. They need the Sun for their life energy. Why did I not think about this earlier?*

He instantly ordered the bee, 'Fly fast, my bee. Only Sussaina can give me a solution. She cannot let her people die. Yes, she will give me a solution!'

A strong wind blew on Drudan's face, and he yelled in pain. Moonlight had distorted his face so much that even the touch of the wind hurt him. He cried aloud, 'Damn the Moon and damn Sussaina!' He bent low on his stomach, his face literally touching the bee's back. After some time, the milky illumination of the Moon was replaced by darkness, which grew as Drudan proceeded ahead.

From a distance he could see a lady sitting in dark, only the glow on her face provided some illumination.

As Drudan approached closer, he called out, 'Oh, my queen Sussaina looks miserable. How was your trip to Zynpagua? My apologies for capturing you back. How dare you escape from here!'

Sussaina turned towards Drudan and said, 'Finally, you could gain some courage to come and see me. What happened to your face?'

When Drudan did not speak, Sussaina continued, 'Don't tell me you could not stand the moonlight again. Isn't it amazing, moonlight calms people but it burns your face? Can you not see the evil inside you? Drudan, my children will end your life one day and before that happens, surrender to the planets and save Zynpagua.'

Drudan laughed. 'Sussaina, I admire your courage. It has been more than ten years since I bound you here with my spell. You look miserable and old yet reluctant to succumb. Sussaina, help me influence the planets and I will free you. In fact I will spare your children.'

Sussaina smiled and said, 'Drudan, you cannot stand the moonlight, then how will you stand the rays of the Sun? Zynpagua is my land, and I will not do anything to harm my people. They are waiting for my return. They know I will come back and save them.'

Drudan began to laugh maliciously and said, 'You will save Zynpagua? You? Have you forgotten that you are in my captivity for the last ten years? Look at yourself, aged and bony. You will save the people of Zynpagua? I must say this is a nice dream.'

Sussaina covered her face with her hands and said, 'You are an evil man and I detest seeing your face. Go away. Let me tell you my children will save Zynpagua. The day Anika wins the favour of Sun and Mars, you will be finished, Drudan!'

Drudan began to laugh viciously. Dancing with joy, he said, 'Your children? Huh! I thought you have been seeing them from here. Don't you know Anika is already dead? My Violet killed your dear daughter in seconds. Ha! Ha! The saviour of Zynpagua dies in seconds. My god, what a feeble saviour was she.'

Sussaina was stunned. She yelled, 'You cannot do that. My daughter is special, you cannot kill her!'

Drudan laughed. 'Your special died like an insect.'

Sussaina tried hitting Drudan, but she was bound by his evil spell. She howled aloud and fell to the ground. 'No, you are lying. It cannot be!'

Drudan was laughing and said, 'Sorry, dear queen of Zynpagua.'

Then he placed his hand on her shoulder and clawed her skin while saying, 'Now listen to me. Help me impress the Sun or else I will kill Vivian, as well. Save your son!'

Suddenly, Drudan's hands began to burn.

Sussaina pushed him away and said, 'Don't you dare touch me! The Moon and stars are angry with me, but they will never let anyone harm me. Don't you dare touch me!'

Drudan blew air on his hands and stopped the burning sensation. He screamed at Sussaina, 'I cannot harm you? Really? I have killed your daughter. Now live in pain and remain here all your life. If you will not support me in influencing the Sun, the people of Zynpagua will die anyhow. You will kill them with your obstinacy.'

Sussaina did not speak but continued to weep. She said, 'My daughter is born with a mission. She will rescue the people of Zynpagua.'

Drudan turned mad with fury and yelled, 'You stupid woman, she is dead! Can't you understand? Check for yourself.'

Sussaina looked towards Zynpagua. She was gifted with a special vision with which she could see things at any distance. That is how she had been following Vivian and Anika. In fact she had been communicating secretly with Frederick also. She tried locating Anika but could see only a burnt house. She panicked, her children were nowhere. Drudan saw the expressions on her face and laughed. 'I told you Anika is dead!'

Chapter 6

Soulmate

The atmosphere was inundated with fumes being emitted from a huge pot filled with wood. Lady Carol was chanting a prayer in front of the fire, in a lonely patch of the jungle.

Anika lay unconscious on the nearby cot. Vivian and Femina were attentively following Lady Carol's instructions.

Femina was racing from Lady Carol to Anika. She was pouring water in Anika's mouth. The colour from Anika's skin had faded. Vultures were circling in the sky, waiting for Anika's soul to leave the body. The violet light intercepted the white protective halo cast by Vivian. It had entered Anika's heart and injured her soul. Vivian was shocked to see his sister collapse that way. He could not believe that Drudan's magic had surpassed the protective spells Pajaro had cast. Drudan had become more powerful since then. When the violet light hit Anika, Vivian instantly carried her with the whirling wind before Violet could attack again and swallow her body.

Lady Carol had witnessed the event from the kingdom of clouds and had descended to save Anika. While Vivian had disappeared with Anika, Lady Carol saved Femina and the fisherman and flew them with her. They had found a clearing in the jungle and were saved by the tall bushy trees that posed a barrier for the violet light to find them. Lady Carol had then cast protective spells on the area. These spells were unique and only some people from the kingdom of clouds could use them. Lady Carol used her spells and summoned Vivian there.

Lady Carol had then instructed everyone to join her in the prayer to save Anika When Lady Carol had checked her pulse, she was sure that Anika's soul was fatally wounded. She had begun to chant a prayer.

She had been doing that for the last four days but had attained no success. Anika's breathing was gradually diminishing. Lady Carol held her head and sat in despair. There was no point chanting further. Anika's life was not reviving. Vivian panicked when he saw Lady Carol had stopped chanting. He cried aloud, 'No, this cannot happen! You must save her!'

Lady Carol's was in tears. 'In some minutes her soul will depart!' she said.

Vivian cried aloud, 'No! It cannot be. She has come to save this world, how can she go like this?'

Lady Carol sorrowfully replied, 'Her soul has been injured! The violet rays have sapped the life from her soul.'

Vivian pleaded, 'Please help her; there must be a solution! She is a special girl and cannot die like this!'

Femina was also weeping. She placed her hand on Vivian's shoulders.

Lady Carol thought for a while and then a flash of hope appeared on her face. She said, 'My grandfather used to say that a dying soul can survive if it borrows life from its soul mate. I have seen him perform this spell only once when I was a child. No one dares to try it because it can risk the life of the soul mate as well. Anika can only survive if she has a soul mate- a boy whose soul she shares. We can cajole his soul to give its life to Anika. But she is very young, and I do not know whether there is a soul mate in her destiny.'

Vivian fell on his knees and begged, 'Please show us the way, Lady. My sister's life can be saved if you will try.'

'Dear son! I do not know how it is done. There are dim memories of my grandfather performing this spell. I was not allowed to enter his room. I remember the spell faintly and can try, but if it backfires, we all can die!' said Lady Carol.

Vivian was emphatic, 'What is the point in leading a life whose purpose is defeated? My existence is pointless if I cannot save my sister. I will end my life, Lady, if anything happens to my sister.' He cursed himself for getting her from India. 'She was safe on the Earth. I got her here. I put her life in danger.' Saying this, Vivian began to sob. He said, 'I don't want to live any more.'

Femina agreed with Vivian and said, 'Lady, we are not afraid of the consequence, just save Anika.'

Lady Carol nodded and said, 'I know, dear. I will try my best.'

She closed her eyes and taking a deep breath, pronounced 'Om!' The sound began to resonate. After some time, Lady Carol's voice began to echo, and it appeared to be coming from the heart of the jungle. She went on calling 'Om' in one breath, without breaking the flow, without stopping for breath. There was a strange vibration in the environment, and then the trees began to shake. Soon the atmosphere was inundated with a strange gurgling sound, and then everything around began to rotate. Femina shrieked at what she saw and caught Vivian's hand. The fisherman covered his face in terror. Lady Carol went on calling 'Om'. Soon the trees around began to spin, the clouds burst, letting out a downpour. The area began to flood. The water level began to rise. When the water level reached Vivian's waist, he rushed towards Anika and lifted her from the cot and held her on his shoulders. When the water level reached their nose, they began to gasp for breath. Lady Carol continued to chant nervously. Vivian lifted Anika and held her above his head. He then stretched his left hand and uttered a spell. Femina, Lady Carol, the fisherman, and Vivian became double in height.

But unfortunately, water had entered Lady Carol's mouth by then and her voice became incoherent. She desperately wanted to halt to take a breath, but she continued, with her voice staggering to maintain the continuity. Drops of perspiration appeared on her forehead and her lips shivered. The environment around was turbulent. Soon the trees began to fall, and a series of lightning inundated the sky.

Lady Carol could not continue any more, and she began to cough, thereby halting her chanting. Femina screamed as Anika turned black when Lady Carol stopped. A thunderstorm blew violently throwing Vivian away from Anika. She fell in the water.

Lady Carol cried out, 'I knew this would backfire. Anika is no more!'

Vivian howled and rushed towards Anika, but a gust of wind blew him away. Suddenly, everything around became still and dark. The water level receded and they came back to their normal heights. No one could see anything.

Vivian ran towards Anika and held her. She had turned cold. Vivian cried aloud, looking at the sky, 'Mother Sussaina, please show me a way. Your daughter is dead. Show me a way, Mother.'

Nothing happened for some time, and then the moonlight began to penetrate through the trees. Before anyone could react, a tiny, white bird came flying from the jungle and sat on Anika's heart.

Vivian rushed towards it, but Lady Carol stopped him.

The bird pecked on Anika's heart and disappeared. Nothing moved for some time, and then Anika shuddered. The black shade from her skin disappeared, giving back her beautiful complexion. She took a deep breath and coughed aloud. Femina ran towards her while Lady Carol thanked God!

Vivian held Anika and cried, 'You are alive! My sister is alive! Thank God she is alive. Thank God that Drudan could not kill her!'

Lady Carol smiled and looked up at the sky. She said, 'Your mother Sussaina has sent the moonlight to save her. I am sure she has prayed to the Moon and saved Anika. My son, your mother has done it again!'

Vivian looked up and said, 'Mother Sussaina, you are the most wonderful mother. You saved Anika!'

Sussaina was weeping. Yes, it was she who prayed to the Moon to connect Anika with her soul mate and save her. She was grateful to the Moon for hearing her prayer.

Anika was gradually gaining consciousness. She smiled at Vivian and touched his face. Vivian was crying. Anika feebly wiped the tears from his face and fainted again. Vivian panicked, but Lady Carol stopped him. 'Anika is fine, son. Don't worry, she is safe now. Let her sleep. Her soul is recouping.'

Vivian placed Anika back on the cot.

Lady Carol touched Anika's forehead and then her cheek.

'Is she fine?' asked Femina.

She nodded and said, 'Yes, she is fine.'

Lady Carol appeared perturbed. Femina came close to her and asked, 'Lady, what is the matter?'

She sighed and replied, 'Femina, the tiny white bird is bothering me.'

'Even I am concerned. Anika's soul mate is a bird?' Femina innocently asked Lady Carol.

Lady Carol smiled and said, 'Of course not! The soul mate would be a human being with traits of a bird.'

'Human with traits of a bird, doesn't this sound strange?' asked Femina.

Lady Carol looked at her intently and smiled. 'Don't worry, darling. Traits of bird a bird could be ability to fly, great vision and so on.'

Femina was much relieved. 'Then what is bothering you, Lady?'

Lady Carol took a deep breath and said, 'The tiny size of the bird is bothering me. It signifies that Anika's soul mate is in trouble and due to sharing of the souls, his life is in danger!'

Vivian had been patiently listening to Lady Carol and Femina's discussion. He enquired, 'Lady, what can be done now? Should we ask Anika to find him?'

Lady Carol patiently responded. 'It is the rule of nature that people have to meet their soul mates by act of destiny. If we inform Anika, they both can die!'

'Then how will we save Anika's soul mate?' asked Vivian.

'The split souls will try connecting, and Anika will discover him. I hope she is able to do that before he dies!' replied Lady Carol.

Their conversation was interrupted by chirping of birds. They were surprised to find seven birds circling around Anika. Each bird was of a different colour of the rainbow. Lady Carol gasped as she saw them. Tears of joy rolled down her eyes. The seven birds pecked on Anika's forehead. One of them came and sat on Lady Carol's hand, then flew away.

Vivian asked Lady Carol, 'Who are these birds? Do you recognize them?'

Lady Carol turned to Vivian and said softly, 'Vivian, I want to speak to you privately.' Vivian nodded in agreement and followed Lady Carol.

Once they had reached a secluded clearing in the jungle, Lady Carol continued, 'Yes, I recognize these birds. They are the angels of the kingdom of clouds. Pajaro had requested them to take care of my grandson Leo. Once Leo disappeared, I did not see them. They have appeared today after years. It means my grandson is alive. There exists a connection between my grandson Leo and Anika. Only time can tell us what this connection is.'

Vivian was very surprised. There existed a connection between Frederick and Anika, and now it seems even Leo was connected to her.

Lady Carol continued, 'My grandson Leo is very special. Powers of Drudan will start diminishing once he faces Leo. No magic can stand in front of my grandson. He is god gifted. Drudan tricked him and captured him from behind. The appearance of seven birds has testified that Leo is alive. I am very grateful to God for saving him. Vivian, we must find him. He can play a major role in defeating Drudan.'

Vivian thought for a while and said, 'Lady Carol, how will we find Leo? He has been missing for years.'

'If there is a connection between Leo and Anika, she will find him. But this has to be soon,' said Lady Carol optimistically.

Vivian looked perplexed. 'What connection are you talking about, Lady? Is Leo Anika's soul mate?'

Lady Carol instantly put a finger on her lips. 'Shhhh. Be quiet, son. Anika should not hear this and neither should this news reach Drudan. I am not sure but the appearance of the seven birds shows the soul connection between Leo and Anika. His life is in danger. We have to pray that Anika is able to find him soon. God forbid if anything happens to one of them, the other would die automatically.'

Vivian was appalled at the revelation. 'I won't let Leo or my sister die.'

He began to sob. His entire family had been a victim of Drudan's vile acts. He was desperate to save his mother, find his father, and protect his sister but he lacked the power to defeat Drudan. The thought of Sussaina being pulled back by the violet rays bothered him the most.

He hesitatingly asked Lady Carol, 'Lady, do you think Drudan will kill our mother?'

Lady Carol was appalled by the question. She held Vivian's shoulders and said, 'No, son! He can never do that. Sussaina is a supernatural woman and has the blessing of God by her side. She is paying for her mistake of trusting Drudan, but he cannot kill her. If he even tries, Drudan will be destroyed.'

Vivian was much relieved. He cleared his throat and asked again, 'Lady, do you know about our father? Has he died?'

Lady Carol's eyes filled up with tears, seeing Vivian so distressed. She said, 'Son, no one has been able to trace King Soto. He vanished in the universe. Let us hope that he is alive.'

Lady Carol and Vivian returned after the discussion. Femina, was sitting beside Anika and caressing her hair. Lady Carol warned Femina and Vivian 'Children, when Anika wakes up, do not tell her about the fatal attack of the violet rays. Her confidence would be shattered if she comes to know that violet rays had almost killed her.'

When Anika woke up, she was curious to know what had transpired with her. Vivian gently informed her that she had got injured when the violet rays was taking Sussaina back.

Anika was petrified to hear that. She was awfully scared and nervous. The thought of Sussaina made her worry even more. She asked Vivian, 'How is Mother Sussaina? Has Drudan captured her back?'

Vivian tried hiding the fact from Anika, but when she insisted, he said, 'Yes, sister, Mother Sussaina has been captured again.'

Anika saw the despair on Vivian's face. She wanted to cry out, but controlling herself, she said, 'Brother, don't worry. We will save her from cruel Drudan. No matter what it takes, we will save her.'

Vivian and Anika began to weep and hugged each other. Lady Carol's and Femina's eyes also filled up with tears. Femina held Anika's hand and said, 'We are equal to four hundred people. Nothing can defeat us.'

Vivian smiled at Femina and said, 'Thank you, Femina, but Drudan is very powerful. His violet light enters the blood and can annihilate anyone. We do not know how to fight that.'

Lady Carol immediately spoke out, 'We have to find Leo. Drudan's powers will fade in his presence. That violet light will not be more than a roman candle if Leo comes by our side.'

Anika was listening attentively and asked Lady Carol, 'Leo is your grandson? Did you get any clue to find him?'

Lady Carol hesitated for a moment and said, 'No, Anika, not yet, but I feel we will soon find him.'

Anika did not want to discourage Lady Carol. 'Of course!' said she. Then she murmured to herself, 'How can we find Leo?'

Vivian and Lady Carol looked at each other and then at Anika. They were hoping Anika would soon establish a connection with Leo.

Anika thought for a while and said, 'Brother, I want to be in Zynpagua till we rescue mother Sussaina, but I am worried about my family on the Earth. My sister Radhika would have woken. She adores me and would be very anxious if she cannot find me.'

'Don't worry, Anika. I have left a magical spell in your house. Your parents and sister will continue to sleep till you are back. Trust me, they won't wake up,' said Vivian.

Anika smiled and thanked Vivian. He continued, 'Anika, as mother had warned us, we are facing the toughest time in our life. We can only fight Drudan if the planets are with us. My dear sister, you have already impressed Venus. Once Sun and Mars are by our side, we can rescue our mother.'

'Dear brother, I am trying,' said Anika. She noticed Vivian's stressed countenance and questioned him, 'What is the matter? Are you hiding something from me?'

Vivian lied and assured Anika that there was no problem. How could he have told her that she had to find her soul mate soon or else her life was in danger?

Anika emphatically pledged, 'I swear I will win the favour of Sun and Mars to defeat Drudan. I swear I will rescue mother, even if it takes my life—'

Vivian yelled, 'No, don't talk about taking your life and never say that again!'

Anika found something fishy in Vivian's reactions. She inquired, 'Is something wrong?'

Vivian tried bringing Anika's attention to Leo and said, 'Dear sister, we have to find Lady Carol's grandson Leo. We really do not know how long you will take to impress Sun and Mars. But if we can find Leo, we would have a solution to face Drudan.'

'How will we find Leo?' Anika questioned Lady Carol.

Lady Carol smiled and said, 'Dear Anika, you wish you can find him and God will answer your prayers.'

Anika was finding Lady Carol's and Vivian's reactions very strange. She could sense they were hiding something from her. But before she could ask them, Femina called everyone for dinner.

Post dinner, Lady Carol cast a protective spell, binding the trees of the jungle to guard them. Everyone went to sleep.

As Anika slept, she saw Frederick in her dream. He was weeping and said, '¡Querida Anika, gracias a Dios que estas vivo!' [Dear Anika, thank God you are alive!]

Anika was taken aback to hear that and said, 'Of course I am alive. Why did you say that?'

She immediately repeated the sentence in Spanish, 'Por Supuesto que estoy vivo. ¿Por qué dijiste eso?' [Of course I am alive. Why did you say that?]

Frederick hesitated and, without answering Anika, disappeared.

Chapter 7

The Sealed Prince

When Anika woke up in the morning, she told Vivian about Frederick. She was inquisitive to know why Frederick had said 'Thank God you are alive'. Vivian was very surprised. How did Frederick know about the entire event? The expression on Vivian's face made Anika even more curious, but Vivian distracted her by asking about Frederick.

'Dear sister, could you find out why our uncle Frederick is in Siepra Nevada?' said he.

'No, uncle had got very angry when I questioned him on this,' Anika replied.

Vivian continued, 'I have heard some people of Zynpagua talk about it. They said that Uncle Frederick was our parents' favourite. He was a very kind boy and people of Zynpagua loved him. Then one day he went to the jungle and disappeared. There are rumours that he was cursed.'

Anika was aghast. 'Cursed? Why?'

'These are just rumours; we don't know what happened. But it seems that Uncle Frederick is connected with you. Only you can find the answer to what transpired with him,' said Vivian.

Anika kept wondering why Frederick was in Siepra Nevada and how he was connected with her. She could also speak in Spanish. How, she did not know.

Anika's thoughts were broken by a craving for flying; she stretched her hands and began to run in the open field.

Femina had joined Vivian by then and saw Anika dash forward with stretched hands.

She whispered in Vivian's ears, 'Is this because of the bird's soul?'

Vivian smiled but said nothing.

He knew people from the kingdom of clouds could fly. He had seen Lady Carol fly. He thought, *Maybe Leo flies and therefore Anika is getting this urge to fly.*

He chased Anika and stopped her. 'Sister! Listen.' Anika halted. Vivian continued, 'Dear sister, you are feeling better now. Mother Sussaina had told us to be prepared for the coming days. I think you should commence your training.'

Anika had pledged to rescue her mother and started her practice session at once.

That afternoon was spent in learning sword fighting. Vivian was training Anika. She initially struggled but, by the evening, had conquered the art and was using her sword with agility and aptness. She was very tired, and Vivian gave her a break.

Anika sat down beneath a tree, but the thought of the violet light taking her mother Sussaina began to bother her. She kept thinking of how to impress the Sun and Mars. When she could not get an answer, she went to speak to Lady Carol, who was calmly meditating in the open.

Lady Carol was murmuring something. Anika bent close to her and heard that she was saying, 'Seven angels of the kingdom of clouds, please help Anika connect with Leo. The times are testing and their souls are searching. Help, dear angels, connect them soon.'

Anika was surprised to hear her prayer. She immediately spoke out, 'Connect me and Leo?'

Lady Carol instantly opened her eyes. She turned pale seeing Anika. When Anika repeated her question, she said, 'Darling, you are a gifted girl. I was just hoping that you could find Leo, my grandson, by reading the stars.'

Anika nodded and said, 'I will try, grandma. How old is your grandson?'

Lady Carol said, 'He was four years old when cruel Drudan captured him. He must be fourteen now.'

Anika asked her again, 'Can you give me a clue to find him?'

Lady Carol looked at her and said, 'What clue should I give you, darling, when I have not seen him for the last ten years?' She thought for a while and said, 'Oh yes! He had deep blue eyes. They were a set of the most beautiful eyes I have ever seen.'

The memory of Pajaro and Leo made Lady Carol sad. She looked so much in pain. Anika hugged her and said, 'Don't worry, grandma, we will find him.' She hesitated for a while and then asked her, 'How did Drudan capture him? What had happened?'

Lady Carol narrated the episode, 'When Leo was born, Drudan came to see his child. As he took Leo in his arms, he wailed in pain and became powerless. Even Pajaro was shocked to see that. Then the seven birds of the kingdom of clouds informed them that Leo was a gifted child. The powers of an evil man would fade in his presence. Drudan had become furious at this revelation and wanted to kill Leo. Pajaro was terrified with the way Drudan reacted. She taught him magic to save Leo. Drudan instantly activated the violet light on learning magic. Pajaro tried saving Sussaina and Soto, but Drudan fatally wounded her and took Leo with him. Before Pajaro died, she requested the seven birds to follow her son. The seven birds followed Leo. No one knows where the birds disappeared.'

Lady Carol began to weep while narrating this episode.

Anika consoled her and said, 'Lady, aunt Pajaro died saving my mother Sussaina and brother Vivian. I promise you that I will read the signals sent by stars and discover where Leo is.'

Lady Carol smiled at Anika and said, 'I have full confidence in you, my child.'

Anika was wondering what made her promise Lady Carol. She felt an inner voice was forcing her to make a commitment. She came back to her cot and silently lay on it, thinking about Sussaina's instructions. She had to influence Mars and Sun. How? She did not know. Then the thought of Frederick worried her. Why was he cursed and sent to Siepra Nevada? From the thought of Frederick, Anika's mind drifted towards Leo. How was she connected to him?

So preoccupied was her mind with these thoughts, that she did not realize when she dozed off to sleep.

Anika felt her body turn cold. Her teeth were clattering, and she was shivering. She tried bringing her hands close to her chest but they were frozen in the ice.

She yelled, 'It is freezing here, my hands and feet are tied, please give me water, someone please come. The blood in my veins has dried. I can't breathe! I can't breathe!'

Femina and Vivian were sitting near the bushes in the jungle. They heard Anika's voice and dashed towards her. Anika had fallen from the cot and was lying on the floor, absolutely curled up.

Femina touched Anika's forehead. It had turned ice cold. She screamed aloud, 'Lady Carol, come fast!' while Vivian began to rub Anika's palms.

Lady Carol had been meditating and ran towards Anika. She touched Anika's forehead and said, 'Hurry! Get something warm to drink.'

Femina rushed inside the hut and got some hot soup for Anika while Vivian lifted her and placed her back on the cot. When Femina tried making her sip the soup, Anika shuddered as if someone was passing electric current through her veins. Femina forced Anika's lips to part and slowly poured the soup in her mouth. After a while the convulsion ceased, and she drifted off to sleep.

Vivian was flabbergasted. 'Lady Carol, what is happening to my sister?' he asked.

Lady Carol seemed concerned. She said, 'I don't know what this means, either Anika's soul mate is locked in a place where it is freezing cold or it was the soul mate's last attempt to connect with the soul.'

Vivian was exasperated. 'What do you mean by soul mate's last attempt to connect with the soul?'

Lady Carol was weeping. 'It means Leo is dying.'

Vivian threw his hands around Lady Carol and hugged her. He said, 'It cannot be. My sister is still alive, then how can Leo die?'

Lady Carol continued to weep. 'Son, I don't know anything.'

They had only one option: to wait for Anika to wake up.

That night was spent in praying and pleading to God to save Anika and Leo. Was the soul mate dead? This question was haunting everyone's mind.

After several hours, Anika moved. Femina excitedly pointed out. 'Look, Anika is moving.' Everyone circled around her. Anika's lips moved again, and she called for Vivian. He held her hand and said, 'My dear sister, please wake up.'

Anika was still unconscious and murmuring,

How could a father lock his son?
In a land not known to anyone.
The weather there is icy cold,
He is left there to get old,
His face is sealed beneath the ice,
Inundated with tears are his blue eyes,
The blood is drained out from his veins.
The birds around mourn in pain.
Someone please rescue this prince,
He would be the ruler a province.

Lady Carol hushed everyone, 'Listen carefully, she is talking about her soul mate.' She began to weep again. 'My god! Leo is sealed beneath ice!'

She kept repeating what Anika was saying. Vivian continued to hold her shoulder and pacify her. 'Don't worry, Lady, everything would be fine.'

Anika woke up after sometime. Tears rolled down her eyes, making her pain more poignant. Vivian gently placed his hand on her head and asked softly, 'Dear sister, what happened? What are you murmuring?'

Anika spoke in a state of trance, 'It was a bizarre and a painful dream. There were mountains and glaciers and the wind puffed ice. The land was frozen with snow, and there were no trees. Beneath a frozen lake was a face of a young boy with blue eyes. He could hardly breathe. He has been lying there for years.'

Vivian's face turned pale. He knew this boy could be Anika's soul mate, Leo. Lady Carol was howling so profusely that Vivian had to request her to leave the place before Anika guessed there was something seriously wrong.

Anika continued,' Brother, I am feeling restless as if my soul wants to go and find him!'

Vivian stood speechless. How could he tell Anika that her soul had died and she was living on a borrowed soul of Leo, who was in danger?

He cleared his throat and, without revealing anything, said, 'Anika, I do not know why you are getting this urge. All I can say is that you are special, and if these intuitions are bothering you, then it is an indication. You will have to find this place where Le-er... this prince is locked.'

Anika got irritated, 'It is hot here. How can I find a place where it is freezing cold and the rivers are frozen?'

Vivian caressed her and said, 'Think, my dear sister, think. If you have dreamt about this place, think where you have seen it.'

Anika replied, 'Vivian, I think I should first concentrate on impressing Mars and Sun. How else will we be able to rescue Mother?'

Vivian emphatically responded, 'No! Find this prince. He will die otherwise. Here is someone's life at stake.'

Anika insisted, 'All our lives are at stake, including Mother's! I don't know what to prioritize.'

When Anika saw Vivian was very tense, she asked, 'Is there something you are hiding from me?'

Vivian replied, 'No, my dear sister, but please find this prince!'

Anika did not want to bother Vivian. She knew he was hiding something from her and said, 'Let me sit in peace and think where I have seen these frozen mountain ranges.'

Anika sat separately near a mango tree, while Femina, Vivian, and Lady Carol sat together. When Vivian was consoling Lady Carol, Femina came to know that Leo was Anika's soul mate and his life was in danger. The three sat in silence, hoping Anika could find a clue to reaching this ice studded place.

Vivian kept thinking about the lines Anika was murmuring.

How could a father lock his son?
In a land not known to anyone.

Drudan was the cruel father who had locked his son in an unknown land. He continued to pray to God to show them a way.

Their silence was broken by the sound of someone screaming. Anika came running towards Vivian and told him, 'I know where I have seen these frozen glaciers and lakes. These are in Siepra Nevada near Spain!'

Vivian's face lit up. 'Is this the place where our uncle Frederick is? My dear sister, you must go to Spain at once. Save the prince!'

Anika hesitated and then questioned Vivian, 'Is this how my destiny is linked to this prince? I have to find him?'

Vivian knew the answer but feigned ignorance in Anika's presence. 'Why are we assuming so much? First find the prince.'

Anika knew Vivian spoke curtly only when something bothered him immensely and chose to obey his instructions.

She prepared herself for Siepra Nevada and requested Vivian to get her a jacket, a pair of tight-fitting jeans, and high boots. Vivian lifted his hand and magically created the clothes which Anika desired. She wore the clothes and told Vivian, 'Brother, I will be missing for some days. What will you tell Femina and the fisherman? I am sure Lady Carol already knows that I can reach Siepra Nevada but what about Femina?'

Vivian smiled. 'Don't worry, sister. I will explain it to her.'

Anika went inside the hut. She panicked on not finding the Spanish chocolate. How would she go to Siepra Nevada without swallowing it? She ran outside and called for Vivian, 'Brother, I have lost my Spanish chocolate. How will I travel to Siepra Nevada now?'

Vivian held his head. He had left all their belongings in his house when Violet attacked Anika. He knew Drudan would have destroyed everything. Then how would Anika reach Siepra Nevada?

Anika kept calling Frederick with the hope that he appears, but he did not appear.

After a lot of contemplation, Vivian suggested, 'Anika, Mother Sussaina had mentioned that you have been able to impress Venus. Why don't you pray to Venus to show you the way?'

Anika gladly agreed. She looked up at the sky and saw Venus shining in close proximity to the Moon. She held her hand up and prayed, 'Dear Venus, please help me reach Frederick.'

There was no response from Venus. Anika thought for a while and framed her sentence properly.

My uncle Frederick is in a land far away,
People say he has been cursed for many days,
Then there is this prince confined in ice,
They both have paid a heavy price,
How should I rescue them?
I have lost the mode to reach them,
Kind Venus, show me the way
To reach Siepra Nevada today.

Before Anika could even finish, a thick beam of ray emitted from Venus and fell on her forehead. She vanished instantly.

Femina was coming back after bathing and screamed aloud. 'Anika has disappeared?'

Chapter 8

The Curse

Anika found herself standing on a mountain slope inundated with ice. Frederick was gliding on the opposite slope, when he sighted Anika. He had worn a helmet and a red leather jacket. His eyes were covered with glasses and Anika could not recognize him. He aggressively waved at Anika. When he did not get a response from her, he came closer and said, '¡Hola sobrina! ¿Cómo estás? Ha pasado tanto tiempo desde que nos conocimos.' [Hello, niece. How are you? It has been so long since we met.]

Anika was taken aback by his sudden appearance. When he removed his helmet and glasses, Anika smiled. '¡Tío Federico! ¿cómo estás?' [Uncle Frederick! How are you?]

Frederick smiled and said, '¡Muy Bien, gracias!' [Very well, thank you!]

'Quiero su ayuda' [I want your help], said Anika.

When Frederick nodded in agreement, Anika narrated her dream of the boy sealed in a glacier. She told Frederick, '!Tenemos que encontrar al chico o de lo contrario podría morir!' [We have to find the boy or else he might die!]

Frederick thought for a while and said, 'Por favor, describa el lugar para mí.' [Please describe the place for me.]

Anika narrated what she saw, 'Hay lagos helados rodeados de altas montañas.' [There are frozen lakes surrounded by high mountains.]

Frederick thought for a while and responded, 'Creo que conozco el lugar pero es muy lejos y en una gran altura. Tendremos que planificar antes de comenzar nuestro viaje.' [I think I know the place, but it is very far and at a very high altitude. We will have to plan before commencing our journey.]

Anika stayed in Frederick's cave that night. It was the most peculiar place high on a mountain. Frederick had made a bed of leaves and cotton balls. He told Anika to lie on that while he slept on a bundle of dried leaves. A low-flame lantern was lit towards the closed end of the cave. Beside the lantern, Frederick had made a small fireplace. Tall flames were emerging from it. There was a heap of dried twigs to continue feeding the fire. The inside walls of the cave were beautifully painted. Some photo frames had been placed near one of the walls. Anika went closer and examined the paintings. They were beautiful. She asked Frederick, 'Estos son preciosas. ¿Quién los ha pintado?' [These are lovely. Who has painted them?]

'¡Por supuesto que soy yo. Me gano la vida vendiendo mis pinturas en el mercado local en España!' said he. [Of course it's me. I earn a living by selling my paintings in the local market in Spain.]

Anika turned around to look at the other walls and gasped with excitement. One wall had been sculptured with the image of a woman.

She exclaimed, '¡La imagen de la Madre Sussaina!' [Mother Sussaina's image!]

Frederick smiled and said, 'Si, ella es como mi madre tambien.' [Yes, she is like my mother too.]

Frederick looked at Anika and then continued, 'Madre Sussaina ha estado llamando a mí. Puedo oír su voz. Ella es la que me dijo que fuera a conocerlo en Shillong.' [Mother Sussaina has been calling out to me. I can hear her voice. She is the one who told me to go and meet you in Shillong.]

Anika was very surprised. '¿Madre Sussaina te lo dijo?' [Mother Sussaina told you?]

Frederick smiled. 'Sí, lo hizo. He venido a vosotros con sus instrucciones. De hecho, buscó el favor de las siete aves de reino de las nubes y me mandó a conocerte. Cada vez que tenía que llegar a ti, yo rezaba a los siete pájaros y me encontré cerca de usted. Infact los pájaros me habían dicho que el transporte de mercancías desde Siepra Nevada para que pudieran garantizar usted viaja de vuelta con ellos.' [Yes, she did. I came to meet you on her instructions. In fact, she sought the favour of the seven birds from the kingdom of clouds and sent me to meet you. Whenever I had to reach you, I prayed to the seven birds and found myself near you. In fact the birds had told me to carry goods from Siepra Nevada so that they could ensure you travel back with them.]

Frederick also told Anika that the seven birds had established a connection between Anika and any goods brought from Spain or Siepra Nevada. Thus whenever Anika consumed these goods, she landed in Siepra Nevada.

Anika smiled, she knew her mother Sussaina was standing by them, despite being locked in the shadow of the Moon. The mention of seven birds was sounding familiar to her, but she did not know where she had heard their name.

Vivian and Lady Carol had hidden the fact from Anika that Leo was her soul mate and the seven birds were protecting him. Anika had heard their name while she was unconscious. But the mention of seven birds was triggering an association in her mind.

In a state of trance, she told Frederick, 'Las siete aves usted están ayudando y están protegiendo Leo también. Todos estamos conectados.' [The seven birds are helping you, and they are protecting Leo as well. We are all connected.]

Frederick did not understand Anika's statement and said, '¿Estás hablando a mí?' [Are you talking to me?]

Anika came out of her daydream and said, '¿He dicho algo? Lo sentimos, tal vez, estoy soñando despierto. Soy el tío lo siento.' [Did I say something? Sorry maybe, I am daydreaming. I am sorry, Uncle.]

Frederick smiled and said, '¡No hay problema en absoluto!' [No problem at all!]

Anika continued from where she had stopped and asked Frederick, '¿Lo sabe la madre Sussaina cómo hablar en español?' [Does Mother Sussaina know how to speak in Spanish?]

Frederick laughed and said, 'Por supuesto, ella puede hablar ningún idioma. Usted es su hija y ha heredado esta habilidad de su.' [Of course, she can speak any language. You are her daughter and have inherited this skill from her.]

Anika was very surprised. This was the reason she could speak Spanish.

'¿Puede Vivian también hablar en español?' [Can Vivian also speak in Spanish?] she asked.

'No, sólo ha heredado esta habilidad de la madre Sussaina. Cuando la madre Sussaina estaba transfiriendo sus poderes para usted, esta capacidad fue transferido, así' [No, only you have inherited this skill from Mother Sussaina. When she was transferring her powers to you, this ability got transferred as well], said Frederick.

Anika hesitated and asked the question which was bothering her for a while, 'Querido tío, eras casi las ocho cuando llegaste aquí. Entonces ¿por qué no puede usted hablar en Inglés? Madre Sussaina debe haber enseñado Inglés en Zynpagua?' [Dear Uncle, you were almost eight when you came here. Then why can you not speak in English? Mother Sussaina must have taught you English in Zynpagua.]

Frederick got irritated by this question and said, '¡Eso es porque yo estoy maldito!' [That is because I am cursed!]

Anika held his hand and said, '¿Querido tío, por favor, dime quién te maldijo?' [Dear Uncle, please tell me who cursed you.]

Frederick hesitated but Anika insisted. He narrated the incident.

During the rule of King Soto and Queen Sussaina, Drudan had befriended Frederick. He knew Sussaina and Soto had no children and Frederick was the only heir of the kingdom. He began teaching Frederick every possible bad habit. He slowly poisoned Frederick's mind against Sussaina. Whatever Sussaina instructed Frederick to do, he would do just the opposite. The birds of the kingdom were Sussaina's special friends. They had taught her the secrets of nature and how to read the symbols hidden in the environment. They used to inform her about any evil happening in the kingdom.

Drudan knew this, and wanted to stop the birds from passing messages to Sussaina. He once called Frederick home for dinner and treated him with the meat of birds. Frederick had developed instant liking for the food. Killing of animals was banned in Zynpagua. Thus Drudan secretly taught Frederick hunting. Frederick had developed such acute liking for bird flesh that he began hunting down the birds. Slowly the birds withdrew all the favours extended to Sussaina. They did not inform her about Drudan's conspiracy. Frederick continued hunting birds, and one day killed two white dancing peacocks. Before the peacocks died, they cursed Frederick and banished him to Siepra Nevada–a cursed and invisible land near Spain. This land was known to cultivate evil. Nothing grew there, no trees, no plants, and no habitation. It was an absolutely frozen place, where wind puffed ice. Sun did not rise in this part of the Earth, and thus it remained dark and cold. Drudan knew that when the birds cursed, they send the person to this region, which was untraceable and unreachable.

When Frederick landed here, he was so shocked that he forgot the language he spoke and had turned dumb. Then slowly Frederick picked up Spanish, the language spoken by people of nearby region.

The birds had left Zynpagua after this episode and had gone and settled in the kingdom of clouds. Sussaina tried asking them the reason, but they were so angry that none of them gave an answer. After few years, when Drudan captured Sussaina, the birds realized their mistake. The seven angel birds told Sussaina about Frederick and his curse. Sussaina pleaded to the angel birds to help Frederick absolve his curse. The birds told her that his curse could only be absolved when the glacial region of Siepra Nevada gets inundated with trees and becomes suitable for birds to live in.

Anika was stunned to hear this. The Siepra Nevada region was capped with snow with no sight of even a leaf. Then how would Frederick's curse be absolved? She panicked.

Frederick saw her expression and said, 'Querida Anika, sé lo que estás pensando. He renunciado. Durante los últimos quince años, he intentado todo lo posible para cultivar árboles aquí, pero está justo al lado de imposible. No creo que mi maldición nunca puede ser absuelto.' [Dear Anika, I know what you are thinking. I have given up. For the last fifteen years, I have tried every possible way to grow trees here, but it is just next to impossible. I don't think my curse can ever be absolved.]

Anika had heard rumours about Frederick's curse but was shaken to hear the same from Frederick himself. Getting rid of this curse seemed impossible. But a thought gave her some hope. Mother Sussaina had been directing Frederick to reach out to Anika. Maybe she had a solution.

Frederick wanted to avoid any further discussion on this topic and left Anika in the cave and went to the Spanish marketplace to buy goods for the journey. He returned late in the night, carrying with him a pair of gloves, boots, jacket, cap, skis, and goggles for Anika. He also brought a basket full of pomegranates for them to eat. They sat in the night and made a plan to climb the high mountains of Siepra Nevada in order to reach the glacier and the frozen lakes.

The next day was spent in training Anika on skiing. This skill would facilitate in covering long frozen distances in a short time.

Anika learnt skiing in no time. Frederick thought she probably had inherited this ability as well from Sussaina. After the day's session, Frederick pulled out some bread, cheese, and a bottle of milk from his bag. He boiled the milk and made hot chocolate for Anika. The hot chocolate with thick enticing foam on the top was so appetizing that Anika gulped one glass and demanded for another. Frederick ensured that Anika's stomach was absolutely full before she slept in the night. He knew the journey in the coming days would be very arduous, and he wanted Anika to gain energy for it.

They woke up before daybreak, when dawn was setting in. While the sun never rose here, the mornings were not as dark as the night but a little brighter. Frederick instructed Anika to wear layers of clothing to escape frostbite and the icy wind. Together they stepped out of the house, dressed for skiing, with the bag of clothing and other necessities hung on Frederick's shoulders. Anika had worn her jacket, woollen stretch pants with boots, and tinted shades. Her head was covered with a woollen cap. Frederick had worn his red jacket over a black jersey and black woollen stretch pants over which he wore boots. Anika looked at him and smiled. Her uncle was very handsome. The memory of life in India filled her with nostalgia. She would have flaunted Frederick and Vivian to her friends in India. Those girls had developed a new liking for good-looking grown-up boys. Her sister Radhika had laughed about it and had said it was all a part of growing up.

'Anika, ¿qué estás pensando? Vamos a empezar.' [Anika, what are you thinking? Let's start.]

Frederick's voice brought Anika back from her thoughts. She felt a pinch of pain remembering her sister Radhika and the carefree life in India.

Frederick instructed her to start skiing and take the lead. She initially struggled and went somersaulting several times on the snow-covered slopes. Frederick continued to encourage her till she gained confidence and glided ahead smoothly. By evening they had not reached the point from where Anika and Frederick had to trek upwards towards higher altitudes of the mountain. Anika's stomach churned with hunger, and her body ached with fatigue. She told Frederick that she could not pull it any longer. Night darkened the place around, and the two fumbled for visibility. Frederick held Anika's hand and led her towards a huge hollow in the mountain. It was big enough for them to sit in, avoiding the hostile cold and wind. After Anika sat there, Frederick took out the dry twigs from his bag and lit the fire. They took off their boots and warmed their hands and feet which had turned numb and rigid in the cold.

Anika was removing her jacket when she got another attack. Her mouth remained open, and she froze in her place. She felt a huge boulder of snow trying to enter her mouth. Frederick saw her neck turn red and blue, as if something cold and hard was trying to force its way through the neck. Anika's eyes overturned and she fell flat on the snow. Frederick panicked, not knowing what to do. He ran and collected some snow and put it in the pot that he had carried with him. Then he placed the pot on the fire to melt the snow. It took ages for the water to boil. Anika lay on the ground motionless. Once the water was boiling hot, he poured it in a cup and, in small portions, continued pouring it in Anika's mouth. Her neck straightened, and she inhaled deeply. After some time, she relaxed, feeling better but weak.

Frederick was nervous and trembling. He asked her about the fit. Anika told him that she did not know why such fits were coming. However, when the violet light had hit her, she was unconscious for four days. When she came back to her senses, she had found Lady Carol and Vivian very tense. She felt they were hiding something from her. After some days, she had got a similar fit in which she had seen a young boy sealed beneath the glacier. Vivian and Lady Carol had forced her to think about the location of this boy, and Anika had realized that it was in Siepra Nevada range near Spain.

Frederick was shocked to hear this revelation. Tears of joy rolled down his eyes, and he cried aloud, repeating the words, '¿Por qué esto no me parece? ¡Gracias madre Sussaina, gracias!' [Why did this not strike me? Thank you, Mother Sussaina, thank you!]

Anika was taken aback by his reaction and asked him what the matter was.

He told Anika that when Mother Sussaina got trapped in the shadow of the Moon, she saw Frederick from there and was traumatized to find him cursed. She had begged to the Moon to absolve Frederick's curse. The Moon had foretold that it was destiny's plan and that a ten-year-old girl would come as his saviour. When Sussaina had asked the Moon how she would know that Frederick's curse is gradually absolving, the Moon had told him that this girl would be hit by a violet light and then she would come to Siepra Nevada in search of a boy. Pardoning of Frederick's curse was connected with helping this girl. The Moon had said that if they are unable to find this boy, Frederick would remain in Siepra Nevada all his life.

When Mother Sussaina had wept on this revelation, the Moon had said that Frederick's curse was a blessing in disguise for their family.

Frederick was weeping and saying, 'No me di cuenta de que era usted quien había venido a salvarme. Usted es que diez años de edad, niña.' [I did not realize that it was you who had come to save me. You are that ten-year-old girl.]

Anika was dumbfounded. Everything in her life was predestined. Poor Frederick's curse was also a blessing for her? She felt guilty of causing so much pain to Frederick. It was because of her that he was in Siepra Nevada.

She instantly murmured, '¡Tio, lo siento!' [Uncle, I am sorry!]

Seeing Anika's countenance full of guilt, Frederick said, 'Somos una familia y ésta es nuestra batalla.' [We are a family, and this is our battle.]

Anika wondered how these mysteries were wound up like a puzzle, interconnected, yet unfathomable.

Frederick affectionately ruffled Anika's hair. Placing his hand on her shoulder, he said, 'No pienses tanto. Tome un poco de descanso, tenemos un largo día de mañana.' [Don't think so much. Take some rest, we have a long day tomorrow.]

He went out, gesturing Anika to stretch herself near the fire and sleep.

Several birds were chirping merrily when Anika woke up. She was surprised to find them as the topography was stark, barren slopes inundated with snow with no trace of any birds or animals. When the birds saw her awake, they began singing and circling around her. Frederick could not be seen anywhere. One of the birds, red in colour, came and sat on Anika's shoulder and chirped noisily. Anika was scared stiff. She screamed out Frederick's name but got no answer. The red bird did not move at all; instead, a set of six birds, each of the colours of the rainbow, came and sat on Anika's hands and feet. Then the red bird flew and, after circling around Anika's head, came and sat on her nose, staring straight in her eyes. Bewildered, Anika tried moving her gaze, but it got stuck to that of the bird's gaze. She heard a voice saying, 'The princess has returned!' Anika wanted to say something, but her gaze was transfixed to the gaze of the bird. A tear rolled down the bird's eye and fell on Anika's hand. A flash of light appeared before Anika which showed the image of a very handsome boy with blue eyes. Blood had frozen on his forehead. His skin was pale, and his lips were sealed in ice.

The image disappeared in seconds, and the bird chirped again, this time speaking like humans, 'This is the image of our prince. Please save him. He will die in a day. We have flown miles to reach you, to show you the way.'

Anika had calmed down by then. She found a strange connection with the birds and gently replied, 'Kind birds, I have to reach this prince. Please show us the way, and we will follow you.'

Frederick had joined them and was intently looking at the birds.

The seven birds seemed to have recognized him, and they went and sat on his shoulders and head. The red bird chirped

'The time has come to absolve your curse,
To forget the days which were harsh and worse.
Find our prince
and
Save our province.'

Tears flushed Frederick's eyes and he said,

'Pequeños pájaros,
Muéstrame el camino,
Para deshacerse de mi maldición,
Estoy sufriendo por muchos días'.

[little birds,
Show me the way,
To get rid of my curse,
I am suffering for many days.]

Anika whispered in Frederick's ears, '¿Los conoces?' [You know them?]

Frederick nodded and said, 'Sí, por supuesto, son los ángeles del reino de las nubes y me han estado ayudando a llegar a usted' [Yes, of course, they are the angels from the kingdom of clouds and have been helping me reach you.]

The red bird interrupted their conversation and said, 'We have very little time. Follow us as fast as you can. The violet rays will try stopping us from reaching the prince. Your focus should be on me. The other birds will try distracting the violet light, but you do not follow them. They will fly in the wrong direction! I will lead you to the prince.'

Anika turned to Frederick and asked, '¿Entendiste lo que dijo?' [Did you understand what she said?]

Frederick replied, 'Sí, ella está hablando en dos idiomas.' [Yes, she is speaking in two languages.]

The red bird heard Anika and said, 'Dear Anika, we are gifted in speaking multiple languages. I am actually chirping, but you can comprehend what I am saying in English and Frederick in Spanish.'

Anika excitedly complimented, 'It's a heavenly gift!'

The little red bird chirped again, stating, 'Yes, we belong to the heavens!'

Anika picked the bird from the top of her nose and placed her on the palm and said, 'Sweet little birdie, I will call you angel because you belong to the paradise. Please show us the way!'

The red bird chirped, 'As you say, my princess, follow me. I will fly as low as possible. Do not wear skis now. There is lot of climbing ahead.'

Anika and Frederick packed their belongings and together followed the red bird. The other birds flew with her symmetrically as a group. While walking, Vivian's face flashed in front of Anika. She wondered how he and others would be.

Chapter 9

Drudan's Palace

Femina and Vivian sat outside the hut with their backs resting against one of the trees in the jungle.

Femina asked Vivian, 'What happened in the village today?'

Vivian responded, 'I searched for a job the entire day but failed again. The people are wary of strangers. If I do not get a job, how will I get closer to the people of Zynpagua? Mother Sussaina told me to win their favour. As of now they are scared and weak. No one will support me against Drudan.'

'Don't worry, Vivian, you will find a job soon. What about working in Drudan's palace?' asked Femina.

'Drudan's palace? This suggestion built some hope in Vivian 'Yes, this is a great idea. It will help me know how Drudan works and how much he is torturing the people. Femina, you truly are very intelligent,' said Vivian.

Femina blushed. She loved to hear compliments from Vivian. She smiled and said, 'Learning from you, Vivian.'

Vivian's mind was preoccupied, and without looking at Femina, he voiced, 'But how do I enter Drudan's palace? How is the big question?'

Femina placed her hand on Vivian's shoulders and assured him, 'Dear Vivian, don't worry, I feel God is with us. Despite all odds, he is saving us. See, you were able to save me, and Anika predicted you will be the future king. Anika was able to influence Venus. Soon Anika will find Leo. Our secret team against Drudan is ready. Mother Sussaina will be rescued forever the day Sun and Mars are influenced.'

'Femina, you think all this is easy? I have sent my little sister for such a dangerous task. Her life is threatened and I cannot help her in any way,' said Vivian in a state of desperation.

Femina tried assuring Vivian, 'Of course, you are helping her! You are standing by her in everything. It is her destiny that she is connected to Frederick and Leo.'

'What am I doing myself? Mother Sussaina told me to win the favour of the people of Zynpagua. Look at me. I haven't been able to achieve anything,' continued Vivian, absolutely disappointed.

Femina shook him and said, 'Don't pull yourself down. You have inherited magical qualities from Pajaro. Use them to influence the people of Zynpagua.'

Vivian hugged Femina and said, 'Femina, I am so glad that I met you. You have always given me the right advice.'

'I am older to you. My wisdom comes from my age,' Femina teased Vivian.

Vivian laughed and said, 'For me you are my cute and wise friend.'

Femina blushed. Vivian smiled at Femina, but something made him tense again. His countenance stiffened. 'Will we ever get married?' asked Vivian in a state of confusion.

A jitter of fear entered Femina's veins as well. No one knew what their future was going to be. Drudan was after them, the same man who had imprisoned such a powerful woman as Sussaina. His creation, the violet light, was a fatal weapon. No one had been able to escape death instilled by Violet. Femina got goose bumps.

Vivian noticed the concern on Femina's face. He placed his hand on her shoulder and said, 'Don't worry, we will be fine. If Anika has predicted it, it will be true. She impressed Venus by prophesying our marriage. It will be true, come what may.'

Femina began to weep. The memory of Drudan putting her in jail and then trying to get her married to the oldest man in the village disturbed her. She was grateful to God that Vivian had saved her and that she was to marry him.

Vivian patted her cheeks and held her hand. The two sat in silence for a long time.

After sometime, Lady Carol joined them. She told Vivian, 'Son, I think we should move to the kingdom. We are running out of time. If Drudan finds us, we will be in great trouble. You have to win the people of Zynpagua in your favour.'

Vivian was confused and said, 'Lady, if the commoners recognize us, they will either hand us to the king's soldiers or kill us. We cannot risk it!'

Lady Carol was emphatic, 'Vivian, our future is replete with challenges. We have no option but to face it.'

After pondering for a while, he agreed.

Femina's father, the fisherman, backed out. He was old and fragile and chose to stay in the hut they had made in the jungle. The others thought it was a practical decision. They did not want to risk his life and left him in the hut.

Lady Carol camouflaged herself as an old and sick woman, Vivian as her son, and Femina as his wife. To hide their countenance, Vivian got his hair cropped short. He made an artificial moustache and pasted it on his face with gum. It was a long and curvy moustache, curling upwards towards the end and culminating into a dense bush that covered more than half his cheek. He wore faded clothes and a thick turban on the head. Femina used ash to paint Lady Carol's face with grey lines, signifying old age and illness. Femina wore a yellow tunic and covered her head and face with a veil. Their dresses indicated that they were poor and famished.

Embracing courage, the three marched towards Drudan's kingdom. On entering the main town, they found the streets isolated and the shops closed. From a distance, Vivian could see the king's soldiers dragging a man on the road who was howling with pain. The three hid behind a tree when the soldiers came marching towards their direction. Femina whispered in Vivian's ears, 'What is wrong? Where are all the people?'

Vivian whispered, 'I have a friend who stays near the fields. Let us go to his house. He may be of some help.'

The three tiptoed behind the trees, hiding from the soldiers. After crossing four streets, Vivian heard a painful cry of an old woman. He saw four soldiers were whipping her. One of the soldiers was voicing aloud, 'How dare you come out of the house. The king has ordered no woman can walk on our streets!'

The old woman was sobbing profusely. 'My sons have left me, and I have no food to eat or water to drink. If I will not come out of the house, how will I survive?'

The soldier viciously laughed and said, 'Then die!'

When the man lifted his whip again to flog her, Vivian came out of hiding and held the whip. He fumed. 'Enough!'

Vivian pulled the whip from the soldier's hand and wound it around his neck. Unfortunately, an army of twenty soldiers noticed the brawl and attacked them. Femina pulled the sword from the soldier who was lying on the floor. She then wounded two in sword fighting.

Lady Carol blew some spells in the air and almost ten soldiers fainted and fell on the ground. The remaining soldiers ran away.

When Vivian, Lady Carol, and Femina were about to leave, the old woman came back carrying some water with her. She thanked Vivian for saving her and offered everyone water to drink.

The old woman requested Vivian, 'Son, you have saved my life. Please come with me to my house. I have not seen you here before. Are you new to this place?'

Vivian responded gently, 'Yes, Grandma, we are new here. We cannot come with you because it will put your life at stake. The king's soldiers are after us.'

Femina lifted her veil and bowed to the old woman. The old woman looked at her intently.

She continued, 'Son, I have another house, near the well. I kept it hidden for the fear of my sons taking it from me. Please come with me. If the king's soldiers see us, they will kill Femina!'

Vivian was taken aback and blurted out, 'You know Femina?'

The old woman replied, 'Yes, the king has got her face sketched on every road. Any man who informs the king about Femina will get gold as much as his weight. The soldiers have been asked to kill the fisherman and capture Femina!'

Vivian was shocked to hear that. The footsteps of soldiers alerted them. They hurriedly followed the old woman. Her house was in close proximity to the well, slightly away from other residences. It had a courtyard whose boundary was protected by thorny shrubs. A cow was tied to one end of the courtyard. The old woman requested Vivian to fetch some water for the house. Post cleaning the house, Femina asked the old woman if there was any way she could talk to the girls of the village. The old woman told her that every morning the ladies come to fill water from the well.

Femina was relieved; at least there was a chance to meet the women of the kingdom.

She woke up before dawn and went to the well, disguised as a married woman with her face covered with a veil. As she approached the well, she saw several women with veiled faces, standing in a line to fill water.

Femina stood in the line. She uncovered her face and said, 'Zynpagua has a history of giving birth to the most beautiful women, but alas, the only lady I have seen here- is me.'

The ladies began to laugh. They gradually removed the veils from their faces. Every woman was exceedingly beautiful and attractive.

Femina continued, 'Wow! You are so good-looking. I have also heard that the women of this kingdom were very good in mathematics and could even use swords and ride horses!'

The other women looked at her in amazement. One said, 'Really? We have never got the chance to learn all this.'

Then another woman said, 'You know, one day I opened my husband's calculation book and discovered he had been making mistakes with the accounts. I have not been educated, yet I could understand the calculation.'

The others looked at her in surprise. 'Really?'

Femina cleared her throat and continued, 'Yes, this is true. Women of Zynpagua are special. They can do calculations, use any weapon, and ride any animal. This is the blessing of Venus showered on us due to queen Sussaina's prayers.'

One of the women came forward and said, 'Yes, I know. My mother told me about this. She says that is why Drudan is insecure of the women in Zynpagua. I wish queen Sussaina comes back and saves us from Drudan.'

Femina cleared her throat and said, 'She can come back if we are ready to wage a war against Drudan.'

The ladies looked at her in horror; they hastily went back home. Only two girls, around the age of fifteen, came forward and said, 'We want to rescue the queen.'

Femina hugged them and said, 'Yes, we will rescue the queen! Can you meet me in my house at night? Do you know where I stay?'

The girls nodded and said, 'Yes. We stay next to your house. Let us meet in the evening.'

Post this, they returned home. These daring girls reminded her of Anika. It had been four days, and there was no news from her. Vivian had been going to the jungle every day to check if Anika had returned, but she had not. Lady Carol had tried communicating with her magically, but her attempt failed. Siepra Nevada was on the Earth, way too far from Zynpagua.

When Femina reached home, Vivian had already left in search of a job. Femina told Lady Carol about her experience near the well. Lady Carol was happy to hear that and sat with Femina to make a plan. They had to influence the women of Zynpagua to become stronger and fight against Drudan's evil rule. This revolt was essential to call the heavens for help. No one knew how Anika could influence Mars and Sun. Lady Carol had advised Femina that they would do their bit to help Anika influence the stars. If the women of Zynpagua became valiant again, it would impress the planets in some way.

Vivian relentlessly searched for a job the entire day. He was rebuffed by some commoners while the others shut the door on him. Thwarted and famished, he sat beneath a tree, wondering how to reach out to the people of Zynpagua. A loud cry coming from behind the houses drew his attention. He dropped his belongings and rushed to the place. On a deserted road lay a soldier wailing in pain with his mouth oozing out foam. Vivian ran towards him and sat beside the man. The man indicated towards his feet. Vivian saw two deep black dots on his right leg and at a distance a black cobra wriggling towards the bushes. Vivian immediately understood that the man was bitten by a snake. He took his scarf and wrapped it a little away from bite mark to stop the poison from entering the rest of the body. He placed his mouth on the snakebite and began sucking and spitting the poison out. His lips had turned blue with the venom. After a while, the soldier sat up. Vivian cleaned his mouth and carried the soldier to his house. His wife and children thanked

Vivian gratefully. The man asked Vivian, 'Please let me know if I can be of help in any way.'

Vivian responded, hiding his identity, 'I am very poor, and my family is staying in a house near the well and is starving for the last two days. Please help me get a job.'

The soldier said, 'Dear friend, I do not have fields to give you a job. I work for the king. If you wish, I can get you appointed as the cleaner for the king's kitchen. It is a menial job, but that is all I can help.'

Vivian answered, 'Dear sir, I will be more than happy to take it.'

The man took Vivian to the head cook at the king's palace.

The head cook was a genteel man blessed with a very pleasant sense of humour. His face flaunted thick grey moustaches that hid his lips. His eyes were sagged by the bulges beneath them but twinkled with mischief when he spoke. He must be in his fifties, but his obesity made him look older. He cordially greeted Vivian and instructed him on the chores. Vivian was appointed as a cleaner of the entire palace instead of only the kitchen. The king was miserly towards his servants, and the task of cleaning the palace always rested with only one man. No one managed to stay in the job of a cleaner for long and quit within a week. Drudan did not tolerate if anyone quit the palace. Thus the person was put behind the bars. Fifty such cleaners were already in jail. The head cook had not quit for the fear of going to jail. When he saw Vivian, he pitied him and told him to leave the job. Vivian insisted on taking it.

The head cook relented and told Vivian, 'Gentleman, you will be appointed the cleaner of the palace, which includes cleaning thirty rooms, four balconies, six staircases of fifty steps each, two kitchens, and the king's garden. I wonder how long you would be able to stick to the job. The last cleaner lasted for four days!' He paused to check the expressions on Vivian's face and then continued, 'While the king wants the palace to be cleaned thrice, but experience tells me if you are able to clean even twice, it would be a miracle.' He asked Vivian, 'What is your definition of cleaning?'

Vivian requested the cook to let him know his own definition of cleaning. The cook guffawed. 'Wise man' and then continued, 'Well! The definition of cleaning is the art of sweeping, mopping, and dusting in such a way that one is able to see his face on every article thus cleaned!'

Vivian murmured, 'Now I know why no one wants to do this job!'

The head cook laughed pleasantly and said, 'Young man, I heard you, and yes, you are right. Under no normal circumstance would anyone agree to do this job. It is very difficult to earn your salary here however I ensure you that you will not spend a day without food.'

Vivian instantly developed a liking for the cook and said, 'Please feed me well because I am not going to give up!'

In a spat of laughter, the cook guffawed with his stomach shaking uncontrollably. He patted Vivian's shoulders and took him to the kitchen. He said, 'Son, eat as much as you want to because after this commences a day full of challenges!'

Vivian smiled and bowed his head. Post having some food, Vivian took the broom and commenced sweeping the floor and the rooms, one by one. A very sweet-looking boy was playing in the courtyard. From his attire, it seemed that he was from an affluent family. The boy smiled at Vivian and said, 'Hello!' Vivian hesitated and then smiled back. The boy had been observing Vivian for a while and asked him, 'You are the new cleaner?' Vivian nodded and said 'Yes'. The boy was keenly observing Vivian. He came closer and said, 'You don't look like a cleaner.'

Vivian was shocked by the question and asked the boy, 'Who are you?'

He smiled and said, 'I am Sachinth, the minister's son.'

Vivian bent down and whispered in Sachinth's ears, 'Why do you think I don't look like a cleaner?'

The boy smiled and said, 'You look like a prince to me.'

Vivian was nervous. If a young boy like Sachinth could know he was not a cleaner, then anyone would be able to guess his identity.

Sachinth spoke as if he had read Vivian's mind, 'I may be seven years of age but don't underestimate me. I am good at recognizing people. You definitely are not a cleaner.'

Vivian hushed Sachinth, 'Shhh… someone will hear you.'

Sachinth smiled and said, 'Don't worry. My father is a minister here. No one will try listening to our conversation.'

Vivian tried distracting the boy and said, 'Dear Sachinth, I am a humble cleaner. Please let me do my work, I have to support my family.'

Sachinth smiled, extended his hand and said, 'Friends?'

Vivian smiled but was amazed that a minister's son wanted to be friends with a cleaner. He shook hands with Sachinth and said, 'I have to get back to work now. See you, my friend.'

Sachinth smiled and said assertively, 'Call me whenever you need me.'

'Need me?' murmured Vivian. The boy was trying to indicate something when he stressed on the words *whenever you need me.* The boy was very sharp and mature. Vivian thought *how did the boy guess that I am not a cleaner?*

Chapter 10

The Youngest Queen

Vivian simply ignored the question rising in his mind and resumed cleaning the floors. By the time he had finished cleaning ten rooms, his head throbbed with pain and he felt dizzy. What bothered him the most was that he could not see the reflection of his face in any of the rooms he had cleaned. He paused for a while and went to drink water. The pot of water for the palace servants was kept behind the main veranda. Vivian headed towards it, and while crossing the rooms, he heard someone sob. As he peeped through the window, he saw the king's youngest queen crying. She was a pretty-looking damsel not more than fourteen years of age. One of the ladies was consoling her, 'My dear queen, the king likes you. He will not offer you to Violet. The elder queen died due to her own mistake.'

The young queen was weeping and saying, 'The king married me forcefully. He said that Violet would like to taste my blood. I can only save myself from Violet if Femina gets captured by then. In that case, the king would offer Femina to Violet.'

Vivian's blood boiled when he heard Femina's name. Drudan was after her life. He was disgusted with Drudan and detested the circumstances in which everyone was living. As Vivian moved ahead, he saw another soldier. He had come to drink water. His face was bruised and swollen, and he was spitting blood.

Vivian questioned the man, 'What happened?'

He shook his head, unwilling to reveal anything. When Vivian insisted, he said, 'I am the personal guard of the king. He is eccentric and gets fits of obsession. He wanted me to pluck some mangoes with one arrow. I missed the target, and he whacked me. My friend, stay away from him as much as you can, he is insane!'

Vivian thought, *despite suffering his atrocities, the people refuse to revolt against him. Courage and strength is absolutely missing in them.*

Post drinking water, Vivian commenced cleaning the palace again. It was five in the evening and three rooms, two staircases, and both the kitchens were yet to be cleaned. He was exhausted, and there seemed to be no end to the task given. The head cook came at five and exclaimed, 'What! You have not finished one round of cleaning, what about the second? Young man, your progress is poor. Now come here and clean the kitchens first, I have to cook.'

Vivian spent an hour cleaning the kitchen. Every time he swept and scrubbed, the cook remained discontented and continued pouring water for further cleansing. By the time Vivian finished cleaning, it was already ten in the night. When he went to the head cook, he handed over some food to Vivian to carry home and said, 'Young man, I cannot pay you anything for today's work. You barely managed to clean.'

Vivian's face turned red with rage. Seeing him, the cook said, 'Dear son, I am very sorry, but the king will not pay any wage till he can see his reflection on the articles cleaned. I know it is impossible, and if I will ask for your wage, he will get you whipped. This is my humble way of saving you. Please do not hold anything against me!'

Vivian smiled and said, 'Are you tortured the same way as the rest of them?'

The cook smiled and replied, 'No one has escaped the king's torment. I am only a cook.'

Vivian said, 'Then what is the cure to this misery?'

The cook laughed ironically. 'To start with, clean and make him see his reflection on the floor!'

Vivian smiled and said, 'Tomorrow I shall ensure that the king sees his face in every item I clean, including his own shoes. That is the place where his face should rest!'

The cook hushed, 'Silent boy, no one should hear you or else we are in trouble.'

Vivian exchanged pleasantries with the cook and left for home.

Femina was waiting for him. She ran towards him and hugged him. Vivian gave her the food.

Femina took it and asked, 'Did you get a job?'

'Yes, I did. I am the cleaner of the palace,' replied Vivian.

Femina teased him and said, 'This is great news. You can start as the cleaner and soon become the king of that palace.'

Vivian was very upset and did not respond. Seeing his distraught face, Femina asked him, 'What happened?'

'It was a tough day,' he replied and commenced having food.

While having dinner, he asked Femina, 'Any news from Anika?'

'Not yet, I thought you would have gone to check on her in the jungle,' said Femina.

'I think Anika will be able to locate us here. She has been sent by Venus. The kind star will get her back to the place where we are. I hope she is able to find Leo soon,' said Lady Carol, joining them for dinner.

Vivian assured Lady Carol that his uncle Frederick was with Anika and they would find Leo and save him. While he convinced Lady Carol, he was himself very concerned about Anika's safety.

Post having dinner, Lady Carol and the old woman went to sleep while Femina and Vivian sat in the courtyard discussing the day's events. Vivian narrated what had transpired with him. He told Femina that his task as a cleaner entailed that people see their faces on the floor and walls cleaned by him. Otherwise he would not earn his wage.

Femina's face fell. 'You will never be able to earn a penny and will drain yourself!'

Vivian smiled. 'Yes I know but I have a plan!'

'And what is that?' asked Femina.

Removing the lock of hair from Femina's face, Vivian said, 'I can use magic. Pajaro had said that I could use it only for a good cause. Putting up a fight against Drudan is also a good cause!'

Femina's face lit up with hope. 'It will work, Vivian. I am so sure it will work,' she said.

'I will pray to God to grant me the ability to use magic whenever I need. These are tough times, and I can only win if I am able to do magic and help the people in distress.'

'Dear Vivian, God will surely answer your prayers!' said Femina convincingly.

Vivian rested his head on Femina's shoulders and asked her, 'How was your day?'

Femina narrated the morning episode. Her beautiful and vibrant face exhibited so much hope that Vivian sat up and kissed her on the cheek. 'Thank you for being with me' he said. Femina blushed.

When everyone had gone to sleep, Vivian closed his eyes and prayed to God. It was already half past six when he woke up the next morning. He hurried to the well to take bath and then left for king's palace.

The head cook was standing at the entrance, restlessly waiting for him. On seeing Vivian, he fumed, 'Did I not tell you to report before six in the morning.?'

Vivian apologized.

'The king is in the palace today and wants to humour himself. He will inspect your work. Boy, be prepared for a tough day. No matter what you do, he will humiliate you. All I can say is that, just bow down before him and request him to pardon you,' said the head cook, looking disturbed.

Vivian's face reflected impudence. The man intently noticed his expressions and said, 'Boy, remain humble, otherwise he will whip you.'

'What if I make him see his reflection on the floor that I clean?' asked Vivian with the same coolness.

'Don't dream. It cannot be done!' warned the head cook.

'When does the king want to meet me?' asked Vivian as a matter of fact.

The head cook was concerned with the way Vivian was behaving. He thought Vivian had gone crazy due to the excessive work. The cook tersely responded, 'Noon.'

Vivian thanked him and steadily walked away.

He went to the first room and, standing at its entrance, prayed to God, 'Our father in heaven, please grant me the power to use my magic.'

He tried calling the wind by intently focusing on the northern direction. His excitement grew when he saw a whirlpool of wind approaching him. He calmly instructed the wind, 'Take the dust away from this palace.' The wind gyrated upwards and pulled in all the dust. Vivian then aggressively rubbed both his palms, till they warmed up and itched. He placed the palm on the floor and said, 'Shine!'

The floor, the ceiling, everything in the room, began to shine. Joining his hands, and closing his eyes, he said, 'May you show the image of anyone who comes to see you!'

When he opened his eyes and inspected the floor, he could see his reflection. He looked up, the roof mirrored his image. He ran around to test the efficacy of the cleaning. Everywhere he could see his reflection!

When he was about to proceed to the veranda, he heard a voice, 'Vivian, I have given you the power to use magic, but don't forget, it has to result in saving distressed people.'

Vivian immediately stopped to check the direction from which the voice came and realized it was his own conscience speaking to him. He knew he could only use magic to save lives. He committed himself on doing so and moved ahead.

It was already noon when he reached the kitchen. The head cook said, 'Son! I have requested the king to grant you some more time. Go, run and clean as much as you can!'

Vivian replied, 'I have finished cleaning, take me to the king.'

The cook looked at him intently and asked, 'Have you given up already? Look, son, I understand some more time will not help you in any way, but please remain humble in king's presence.'

Vivian hugged the cook and said, 'Kind and gentle soul, don't worry!' He then proceeded to face the King.

Drudan was seated in a golden chair located at the centre of the main hall. On each side of the king were seated his ministers who were replicating and praising king's actions. Drudan saw Vivian and bellowed, 'Come here, you little ant!'

Vivian moved forward and sat on his knees, bowing in front of the king.

The king raged, 'you insignificant creature, why are you bowing in my presence. You surely have not dispensed your duties well. If that be found, you will be whipped amidst all. I will command the soldiers to shave the moustaches of the head cook for his inability to get dedicated people.'

The head cook stood trembling at the entrance. Vivian flared up with rage, but took a deep breath and calmed down. He began flattering the king and said, 'My lord, the ruler of this kingdom, I am honoured to see you today. My mother always sang songs praising your bravery and narrating the valorous feats you have achieved. My lord, you are the epitome of chivalry and compassion, under your kind rule, the kingdom is flourishing and the people are dancing with happiness.'

The king looked pleased.

Vivian took a note of the king's cheery face and continued, 'Under your rule, my lord, no petition has gone unanswered, no poor has been deprived of food. Everyone has got the reward for what he deserves. My king, I know you are very just and will treat me the way my work deserves to be treated.'

The king was ecstatic listening to his praises and said, 'Yes, if your work is worth a reward, you will get it, young man. But if I find any lacunae, you will bear the punishment that a man should bear who shirks his duties.'

Vivian bent further and said, 'I shall humbly accept what my king decides. I know of many rewards granted to men who impressed the king.'

The king thought, *when did I reward anyone?* But agreeing to Vivian, he continued, 'Young man, ask me for a wish and if I am impressed, you shall have it!'

Vivian continued, 'My lord, I want to be your personal soldier and bodyguard.'

The king was flabbergasted and so were the others present in the room. The soldiers whispered to each other, 'He has asked for a curse instead of a wish!'

The king let out a burst of laughter and said 'Very well' and then maliciously continued, 'You can be my personal guard after finishing the day's chores as a cleaner.'

Vivian bowed down and said, 'Long live the kind king.'

The king ordered Vivian to show him the rooms that he had cleaned. Vivian led him while the others followed behind. As the king opened the door to the first room, he was enraptured. The floors, the ceiling, the windows, the decoration pieces—all were dust-free and shining. One could actually see his image reflecting on each item. The king concealed his pleasure and said, 'Yes, this is fine! What about the other rooms?'

Every room and veranda was spotless. The king was impressed, but his notorious mind could not let go. He said, 'I want to see the image on my shoes. Let me see how you clean them.' Vivian joined his hands and sat in front of the king. He rubbed his hands vigorously and then wiped the king's shoes.

The king peeped down to check his reflection. His inquisitive face was clearly visible on the cloth-woven shoes. He was thrilled seeing his reflection, but then a minister standing in close proximity to the king whispered, 'How is he able to create reflection on a cloth shoe? He is doing magic!' The king's face contracted, and shrinking his eyes, he looked again towards the shoe.

'I am impressed with your work, however being a personal guard to the king is a great honour. I want to check your work for seven days and then grant you the wish,' said Drudan, the king.

He then instructed the head cook, 'Take him away to your kitchen and feed him well. I am not interested in shaving your moustache. You will look very ugly without them. I cannot tolerate any hideous sight around me.'

The cook bowed and left. Vivian followed him. When they had left the hall, Drudan ordered his soldiers, 'I am wary of this man. Keep a close watch on him and report any suspicious activity! We have to be alert; he could be a wicked magician. If you cannot keep track of him, I will have to use Violet!'

Back in the kitchen, the head cook was thrilled by the day's activity. He patted Vivian and said, 'Very well, my son, you were able to impress the king, but how did you do that?'

Vivian whispered, 'Magic!'

The cook gaped at him blankly. 'Stop kidding me, boy.'

Vivian smiled and said, 'Seriously.'

The cook panicked. 'No, son! Don't say that, if the soldiers hear this, you will be killed.'

Most of the other servants in the palace had come to know that Vivian had impressed the king. They instantly befriended him, and Vivian got lot of information from them. Drudan had married close to fifty women by then. Each of his queens had been sacrificed to violet light. There was a story in the palace that Drudan trusted his first wife Pajaro. She was a very kind woman who knew magic. But Drudan felt that Pajaro conspired against him when she gave birth to her son Leo, who had the power to deplete Drudan's abilities, -scientific or magical. Whenever Drudan took his son in his hands, he felt like a cripple. He had developed acute hatred for his son. In fact, he tried killing him, but Pajaro intervened. When Drudan created violet rays through his scientific expertise, Pajaro suspected that Drudan was planning something dangerous. The day Drudan activated the violet light, it was Pajaro who sent counter spells to stop the violet rays from killing King Soto. Drudan's invention had backfired due to Pajaro's spells. The violet rays generated catastrophic movements that separated Zynpagua from the Earth. Drudan knew it was all Pajaro's doing and had hit her so hard that she died. Since then Drudan despised women. He did not allow anyone in Zynpagua to respect them. An old gardener told Vivian that he was present when Pajaro died. She had cursed Drudan that her son would bring his death. Since then no one had seen his son Leo.

Another attendant informed Vivian that the palace was getting ready for another sacrifice. Drudan wanted to activate Violet, and the youngest queen was the target. Vivian felt miserable listening to the news. He headed straight towards the queen's room.

She was surrounded by her maids and looked fragile. One of her maids was consoling her, 'Dear queen, do not worry, I saw a very good dream last night. I dreamt a young man had come and saved you.'

The youngest queen replied, 'Don't give me false hope. Let me be prepared to face my death.'

Determined to save the youngest queen, Vivian knocked at the room and said, 'The king has a message to be delivered to the queen!' The other maids hushed sideways, but the head maid questioned him, 'What do you want? No man can speak to the queen directly. Tell me what the king has conveyed.'

Vivian refused to budge being unsure of the intentions of the maids in the palace. He said, 'The king has given discrete instructions, I have to inform the queen privately!'

The youngest queen sat up and ordered the other maids to leave the room. The head maid hesitated, but the queen warmly convinced her that she would be fine. As the maids left, Vivian joined his palms and bowed before the queen. He said, 'Lady, I am only a cleaner in the palace. But I am determined to save you.'

The queen replied sadly, 'Dear brother, why are you risking your life for me? I have no escape but to face my fate!'

Vivian continued, 'Dear queen, I can save you. Please help me rescue you. Drudan cannot go on killing his wives.'

The queen was not sure whether this was another game played by Drudan. She told Vivian, 'Go away!'

When Vivian saw that the youngest queen was not relenting, he spoke a spell and showed his true self to her. The queen was aghast. Vivian saw her expression and continued, 'I am Vivian, the son of king Soto and queen Sussaina. Do you think I will be a part of Drudan's vicious killings?'

The youngest queen began to sob and, joining her hands, bent down in front of Vivian. 'Brother, I want to live. Please save me!'

Vivian held her hand and said, 'You have exactly half an hour. Pack your belongings and wait for me outside the kitchen. Today is your last day of torture.'

The youngest queen began to sob again. She looked terrified and said, 'You will not leave me midway?'

Vivian felt terrible seeing her state and said, 'Of course not. If I do not fulfil my promise, I will die.'

The youngest queen began to cry. She had seen hope after days of torture and despair. She quickly packed her bags and reached the kitchen. It was post lunch, and the kitchen was deserted.

Vivian was standing near the veranda. The queen had tears in her eyes, and wiping them, she said, 'Dear brother, I am ready to leave.'

Vivian cordially responded, 'Let us escape, dear queen. It is time for you to find your freedom.'

The queen's face was vibrant with hope.

Vivian raised his palm and pointing towards the north-west direction, said 'Come saviour winds'. The gyrating dust storm emerged, enveloping Vivian and the queen in it. The youngest queen gasped for breath. Soon Vivian and the youngest queen began to rotate and disappeared. In minutes they reached home and reappeared. Femina was teaching two girls sword fighting and was stunned to see the youngest queen. Vivian narrated the incident and told her, 'The queen will stay with us. Teach her whatever you can. I have to go back before anyone realizes that I took the queen away.' Stating this, he raised his hand and vanished with the wind.

When he arrived in the palace, everything seemed normal. No one was aware of the queen's disappearance. He silently went to the queen's chamber and spoke a spell, 'All the queen's maids, forget what I had said.' The memory of Vivian's interaction with the queen faded from the maids' minds instantly.

Vivian then commenced cleaning. As he turned, his glance fell on a pillar behind which was a soldier keeping an eye on him. As the day proceeded, the news of the queen's disappearance spread like wind.

The king ordered the queen's personal maids to be presented in front of him. They were trembling. The king roared, 'Where is the queen?'

The maids looked dazed and replied, 'My lord, we are not aware. We cannot remember a thing!'

The king bellowed, 'What nonsense? You have failed in your duties and should be whipped till the last drop of blood oozes out from your body!' He commanded his soldiers, 'Whip them now, and I want to see streams of blood flowing here.'

Everyone was stunned. Six soldiers walked in with whips to flog the maids. They pulled their hands up and rotating the whip in the air began spanking the maids. Vivian felt guilty and could not stand the sight. He looked at the whips and whispered, 'Become as heavy as iron.'

The whips became so heavy that the soldiers were not able to lift them. The ministers looked confused as the soldiers halted suddenly.

The king yelled, 'Quiet! Soldiers, pull the whip and hit.'

The soldiers tried with full force, but the whips could not be pulled. Drudan was furious. He thought the soldiers were trying to save the maids. He pronounced an evil spell which turned the maids and the soldiers into statues.

Drudan yelled and ordered another group of soldiers, 'Go and find the youngest queen wherever she is and get her here. Her head will be chopped amidst all and sundry. If you cannot find her by evening, be ready to die yourself!'

The soldiers panicked and left in haste. The rest of the audience dispersed silently after another day of horror and showdown. It had become a regular feature in Drudan's palace; however, every time the punishment was different.

As the people left the hall, Vivian took out a cloth from his pocket and began cleaning the floor which had some drops of blood. He did not want to show Drudan that the day's incidence had affected him. Drudan pretended that he was busy talking to his ministers, but his eyes were stuck on Vivian.

When it was late in the evening, Vivian left the hall and headed towards his house. He must have crossed a mile when he realized that there were two soldiers secretly chasing him. He continued to pray that the queen was indoors and disguised. When he entered the road leading to his house, he saw Femina standing outside, drying clothes. Her face was covered with a veil. Seeing her, he dashed towards her and hugged her. Femina blushed, but then Vivian whispered in her ears, 'Go inside and hide the queen, two soldiers are following me.'

Femina ran in and requested the queen to sit inside a huge drum. She then covered the drum with clothes.

Chapter 11

The Revolt

After some time, four other soldiers came towards Vivian's house and ordered, 'We have to inspect your house, the youngest queen is missing, and we have to ensure that you have not kidnapped her.'

Vivian humbly bowed and said, 'No, I have just come back from the palace.'

The soldiers insisted, 'Even then as per king's orders, we have to inspect every room.'

Vivian shook his head, mentally praying for the queen to be safe. The soldiers rummaged the house and even entered the room which had the drum. One of them tried opening the drum. Femina panicked. Seeing Femina, Vivian gradually raised his hand and, pointing towards the drum, said, 'Open not.'

The soldier tried opening the lid of the drum but could not. He called his colleagues, but none could manage to lift the lid. Vivian cleared his throat and said, 'The lid has been stuck for many days.'

The soldiers kept trying to open the drum. No matter how hard they tried, they could not open it.

At last one of them suggested, 'Let us take it to the palace.'

Vivian pulled Femina to one corner and whispered in her ears, 'You escape with Lady Carol, the queen and the old woman through the back door. I am going to stop these soldiers. Don't come behind me but wait for Anika's return. Even if I am captured, she can influence the stars and save Mother and Zynpagua. I have to save the youngest queen and for that I have to make these soldiers unconscious. I am sure if these soldiers do not return; Drudan will get suspicious and send an army to capture me. Everyone who has helped me will be in trouble. Femina, if you can, influence the people of Zynpagua to stand against Drudan. In the meanwhile, let me face him.'

Femina began to cry. She told Vivian, 'We can fight these soldiers together and then all of us can go and hide in the jungle.'

Vivian emphatically instructed Femina, 'No, I can't do that. Drudan is crazy; he will get the soldier who got me this job, killed. He may also kill the kind cook. I am son of King Soto and Queen Sussaina. I cannot let any innocent man die. Please listen to me, Femina. Take the youngest queen and run back to the jungle.'

Lady Carol agreed with Vivian. She told Femina, 'Vivian is right. Let him go. In the meanwhile, I will help you influence the people of Zynpagua to fight against Drudan. We need people to side with us, and we also have to wait for Anika's return. Femina, do what Vivian is saying.'

Femina nodded. Vivian went back to the soldiers and said, 'Let me carry the drum for you.'

One of the soldiers looked at Vivian suspiciously and said, 'No, we can manage.'

Vivian nodded and retreated back. He fixed his gaze on the drum and said 'Heavy'.

Two soldiers tried lifting the drum but could not. They grew even more suspicious. Vivian thought that there was no point dodging them. He went closer to one soldier and, looking in his eyes, said 'Sleep'. The soldier instantly fell on the ground. Seeing him fall, the other soldiers surrounded Vivian. Lifting his hand, Vivian spellbound some, with whom his gaze met, and punched the others. Soon, the entire group of soldiers was lying on the floor. Once he was sure that the soldiers were unconscious, Vivian opened the drum and asked the youngest queen to come out from it. She was trembling with fear. He assured her that she would be safe with Femina and Lady Carol. He instructed Femina to leave immediately. Lady Carol held Femina's hand on one side and the youngest queen's on the other. She told Femina to hold the old woman's hand so that they could fly in a chain. She commanded 'Lift'. The four of them slowly lifted in midair. The youngest queen exclaimed in surprise while the old woman was shocked to say anything. Without further delay, Lady Carol ordered 'Fly!' They were seen soaring up in the sky and vanished from the scene.

Vivian tied the numbed soldiers with a rope and locked them in his house. He then hid a small dagger in his pants and left for the palace.

As he walked back in the streets, he saw soldiers spread in every nook and corner. One of them even stopped Vivian and asked him why he was returning to the palace so early. Vivian simply lied and said that the head cook had called him early. The soldier let him go, but from their faces, it seemed that they were suspicious of him.

As Vivian reached the palace, he was shocked to see the scene there. One of the ministers had been killed. The head cook did not divulge any information on what had happened; in fact no one was ready to reveal anything. Drudan had left for an urgent tour of his kingdom. The militia had been asked to be very attentive, and the guards had been doubled in the palace. No one was allowed to go home. Drudan had instructed his soldiers to kill anyone they found suspicious.

Vivian was worried. What had caused such a sudden change, and where was Drudan? Was there any threat to Femina's life and others with her? He knew that Lady Carol had cast protective spells in the jungle, and it would be difficult for Drudan to reach them, but even then.

His thoughts were interrupted by the head cook. He instructed him to commence cleaning the palace. Vivian noticed that his face was swollen. He asked him what the matter was, but the cook did not say anything. However, he looked very sad. Vivian grew very tense by what was happening around. He quietly commenced cleaning the floors. After some time, he saw the minister's son Sachinth Goel playing in the courtyard. Vivian secretly walked towards him and asked him, 'What is the matter today? Why is everyone so tense?'

Sachinth smiled. One of the soldiers was passing by and stopped when he saw Sachinth speak to Vivian. Sachinth spoke aloud, 'Clean the dust beneath my feet.'

Vivian instantly bent down to avoid the soldier and cleaned the floor near Sachinth's shoes. Sachinth whispered in Vivian's ears, 'Meet me in the garden.'

Vivian was surprised by the little boy's courage. He met Sachinth in the garden. Sachinth came very close to Vivian and said, 'You are King Soto's son, aren't you?'

Vivian was astounded by the question. How did a seven-year-old boy recognize him? Sachinth spoke as if he had read Vivian's mind, 'My father worked as a minister with King Soto. He has a picture of King Soto. You look exactly like him. That is how I recognized you.'

Vivian did not respond. It could be a trap. Sachinth saw Vivian's expressions and said, 'I know you will not trust me now. I have news for you. My father was telling mother yesterday that Drudan left in haste to a place called Siepra Nevada. His violet light informed him that a young girl has located his son and is trying to save him.'

Vivian panicked and said, 'Oh my god, Anika's life is in danger!'

Sachinth curiously asked him, 'Who is Anika?'

Vivian smiled and said, 'Brave boy, I will let you know one day, but I have to leave now.'

When Vivian turned to leave, Sachinth called out, 'I have information for you.'

Vivian asked Sachinth, 'And what is that, dear brother?'

Sachinth came closer and said, 'While my father is forced to work for Drudan, he has always been loyal to King Soto. He told me to let you know that he and a few ministers are with you in your fight against Drudan.'

Vivian thanked the fearless boy. He wasn't sure if there was a trap in what Sachinth said and therefore did not comment, but mentally he was glad that some people had the courage to stand against Drudan.

The thought of Anika made him very anxious. Drudan had left for Siepra Nevada. He prayed for Anika's safety. Vivian had got so tense listening to this news that he could not work. He held his head and sat on the stairs.

'My son, don't worry, Anika will be fine. Frederick is with her. She will be fine my son. Use this opportunity to win over the ministers' Sussaina's voice alerted Vivian.

Vivian looked up and said 'Mother, is that you'

Sussaina's voice said 'Yes my son. I can see you'

Vivian continued, 'Mother, Drudan has left for Siepra Nevada. He did not spare Leo then how will young Anika face him?'

'Son, the heavens are watching. Anika will be fine. Do not lose this opportunity my boy. Be courageous and win the ministers'

Vivian faced up to respond, but found two soldiers observing him. He immediately stood up and left for the main hall. The soldiers continued to look at him suspiciously.

He went towards the main hall where the ministers had assembled. He knew Drudan was not there, and he could start his campaign against him. He stepped inside the hall and spoke aloud, 'I am Vivian, son of Soto. Without mincing words, let me tell you that I have come to rescue my mother and end Drudan's rule in Zynpagua. Those who want to come with me, step back. Others can prepare themselves for a combat *right now*!'

Four ministers backed out, but the rest ordered the guards to capture Vivian. The soldiers surrounded him. Vivian smiled and said, 'I have not come to be defeated.' Raising his hand, he said 'Sleep!' All the soldiers and ministers dozed off to sleep. The ones who had backed out were spared. Then Vivian tied the sleeping soldiers and ministers with a rope.

He looked at the four ministers. One of them resembled Sachinth, and he guessed the man must be his father. It seemed the man had read Vivian's mind because he came forward and said, 'My son Sachinth told me about you. We are very happy that you have come. Vivian, my son, we are with you in your fight against Drudan. He has gone to Siepra Nevada. This is the right time to turn people to our side.'

Vivian thanked the ministers. He went with them to the town to talk to people and motivate them to stand against Drudan. Wherever Vivian went, people looked up to him with hope. They felt Vivian would save them from Drudan. An old man asked Vivian, 'What about the violet light? Do you know how to fight it? Even your parents could not escape its assault.'

Vivian did not know how to answer this question. The people of Zynpagua were looking at him with hope. How could he say that he had no solution for the violet light? He thought for a while and said, 'My sister Anika has come back from the Earth. She has my mother's power of influencing the Sun and stars. She has gone to Siepra Nevada to save Drudan's son Leo. Let my sister return, the Sun will shine in Zynpagua and then anyone can fight the violet light.'

The people began to weep. They were ready to support Vivian. But their bodies were fragile and weak. Without sunlight and proper nutrition, they had become bones. Vivian knew that Drudan had kept the people famished so that none could have the strength to revolt against him. Without sunlight, the people had developed serious infections. At that moment the only help Vivian could render was to provide them with good food. He raised his hands and called for food. The roads of Zynpagua got lined with delicious meals. People jumped with joy and ate till their stomachs were full. They thronged behind Vivian, singing songs for King Soto and Queen Sussaina. Zynpagua seemed to be in a spirit of celebration.

Chapter 12

Saving Leo

Anika and Frederick attentively followed the red bird. Several times during their voyage, they felt the hostile winds tear their skin and impede their advancement, but as advised by the red bird, they continued to follow it. The other birds would disappear in between and after some time unite, each flying in a line adjacent to the red bird.

The ice-cold terrain accompanied by thundershowers dampened Anika and Frederick's morale. They were shivering in cold. Anika had turned weak and blue. The entire day they walked behind the birds, on the uneven mountain terrain, sometimes down in the valley, crossing some hidden caves, sometimes climbing tall peaks, and then sliding on the slopes. It appeared to be a never-ending journey. The ripping winds, the chilling cold, the hostile frost sapped their energy, and yet they continued to walk, being absolutely aware that delay of even a minute could be dangerous for the prince. Anika had fallen several times during their arduous walk; once she even hurt her forehead, with blood oozing out in spurts and coagulating on the forehead like a dirty mound. Frederick attended to Anika's wounds and feared that Anika was staking her life in the attempt to save the prince.

Dusk was seeping in signalling the end of the day. Anika was exhausted and out of breath. She held Frederick's hand and said, '¡Por favor espere!' [Please wait.]

Frederick called out, 'Estimado pájaro, por favor espere. Mi sobrina está muy cansado.' [Dear bird, please wait. My niece is very tired.]

The red bird flew down and sat on Anika's shoulder. She had tears in her eyes and requested Anika, 'My dear Anika, if we wait even for a minute, our prince will die!' Anika realized that the setting day was fading with a bluish glow, stirring a melancholic feeling within her. She proceeded ahead, asking the red bird, 'How far is the prince from here?' The red bird showed the mountain peak adjacent to the one they were climbing. 'There!'

Anika was aghast. 'That is so far. The sun will set in an hour. How will we make it?'

The bird paused for a minute and then said, 'Dear Anika, we can reach there in an hour if you and Frederick can run.'

Anika and Frederick looked at each other in disbelief. They could hardly manage to walk and now were being asked to run. Seeing their expressions, the red bird continued, 'Dear Anika, we seven birds will combine our energy and push the wind in your direction. When you run, the force of the wind will hasten your speed.'

Anika and Frederick agreed and, holding each other's hands, ran in the direction of the mountain peak where the prince was. The seven birds formed a line behind them chirping loudly and clearly.

Winds of north and south,
Blow the air from your mouth,
Lead Anika and Frederick to the mountain peak,
Where lies our prince with life bleak,
Lift the saviours with your force,
Energize their legs with your source,
Make them run like a horse,
On this land which is so coarse,
Lead Anika and Frederick to the mountain peak,
Where lies our prince with life bleak.

The wind came howling from behind, pushing Anika and Frederick to race like a horse, with legs electrically charged and activated to catch up with the momentum. Their faces turned numb in the speeding air, the mountain peaks, and the adjoining surroundings raced behind in minutes. All of a sudden the wind seized and both dropped on the ice-laden floor. Thousands of birds were circling around a frozen lake; some were hitting at the floor with their beaks, trying to break the ice sheet. The red bird descended and told Anika, 'Please run. Our prince lies there. He is about to die!'

Frederick was the first to stand up and run towards the ice sheet. He froze, seeing the sight of the prince. He was a young boy sealed beneath the frozen lake lying horizontally, with his legs and hands embedded in the layers of ice; his skin was pale and rough as it seemed blood had oozed out from it. His eyelids were partially open which revealed a reddish bluish gleam in the eyes. His warm breath was creating few patches of frost on the floor of the lake; however, his breathing was rapidly decreasing. Frederick yelled, seeing the sight, and came running back to pull out an axe from his bag. He did not notice Anika lying beside the bag, taking deep slow breaths and writhing in pain. Frederick rushed towards the prince and, with all his strength, hit the floor of the frozen lake. Nothing happened. He continued hitting at the lake and finally made a small dent in the ice. He then thrust his hand through the hole and strained his fingers to somehow touch the prince's face. He felt his nose, which had stopped emitting any breath. Frederick panicked, and when he turned around to call Anika, he saw she too was lying still. He ran towards her and lifted her. She was still breathing, but her breath came in sporadically, breaking with long pauses. The red bird stood nearby, crying, and the other birds too descended, mourning and weeping. Frederick felt dizzy, and held his head. Suddenly a thought gave him hope. If Anika was destined to save the prince, he should carry Anika till where the prince was lying. He picked Anika in his hands and rushed towards the lake. He then thrust Anika's hand through the hole on the lake ceiling, trying to touch the prince's face with her hand. As Anika's fingers touched the prince's face, there was a crackling sound, and the frozen ceiling of the lake creaked and sank down. The water of the lake began to melt, and gradually the ice transformed into water and began to flow. The boulder of snow beneath Frederick's feet moved, and he jumped towards the snow-laden ground. Anika toppled to one side and was swept away by the water. The body of the prince moved as well, flowing with the lake. Frederick was frightened at the sight of melting ice and the expanse of flowing water. He took off his clothes and, despite shivering in the chill, jumped in the lake which was carrying both Anika and the prince. He caught the prince first and was taken aback by the warmth in his body. He was breathing normally now, and his hands and feet had become warm, though he was still unconscious. Frederick pulled him out and then placed him carefully on the banks of the lake. He jumped again and vigorously swam to reach Anika, then caught her hand and yanked her towards him. Post placing her on the side of the lake, he too dragged himself out. His limbs ached in the biting cold. He slowly crawled near Anika, who lay unconscious, and began rubbing her feet. After a while, Anika feebly whispered, 'Frederick!'

He was relieved and said, 'Querida sobrina, el Príncipe está aquí.' [Dear niece, the prince is here.]

Anika was feeling dizzy and cold. She had turned numb.

Frederick handed her some clothes and told her to change. Anika changed behind a huge boulder and wore dry clothes. In the meantime, Frederick changed the prince's clothes and made him wear his black stockings, black suit, and fluorescent green coat which he carried in his bag. When Anika returned, she saw Frederick and the prince had already changed. She gaped at the prince in astonishment. In such close proximity lay the most handsome boy she had ever seen, with pinkish fair complexion, black hair, sharp nose, and flawless sparkling skin. He was a tall boy around fourteen years of age.

The red bird flew down and said, 'Thank you, dear Anika. Our prince's life is saved. He is still unconscious. Please wake him.' Tears of joy rolled down her eyes.

Anika touched his forehead, rubbed his hands and feet, but he remained unconscious. Frederick and Anika took turns to rub his palms, but the prince did not wake up. The entire event had been so terrifying that none realized that night had approached, and the dimly illuminated day was replaced by pitch darkness. They could hardly see anything in the frail moonlight. Frederick requested the birds to show him a way to get some wood. The red bird said, 'There is no wood here, we can fly far and fetch some twigs.'

Frederick replied, 'Por favor, haga eso. ¡Gracias!' [Please do that. Thank you!]

He then felt his way to Anika and said, 'Anika, tenemos que encontrar un lugar para encender fuego. El príncipe sigue inconsciente y este entorno y el frío nos engullir pronto.' [Anika, we have to find a place to light fire. The prince is still unconscious, and these surroundings and the cold will engulf us soon.]

Anika was shivering and nodded in agreement. Frederick lifted the prince on his shoulders and proceeded while Anika gathered their belongings and followed. The snow on the ground was knee-deep, inhibiting them from walking, but the only hope to escape the wrath of cold was to find a shelter. After a while, Frederick located a cave towards the leeward side of the mountains and carried the prince in it. It was very wet inside. Frederick made the prince sit on a rock and requested Anika to hold him there while he tried drying the rocks to light the twigs in his bag. He managed to light fire, but the flame was very feeble.

When Anika was holding the prince, she collected her thoughts and tried remembering how Frederick had saved the prince. She repeated the incident in her mind.

> The ice sheet crackled and broke,
> When my fingers touched his nose,
> The temperature was below freezing point,
> Yet the frozen lake melted in no time,
> What caused an entire glacier to melt?
> I cannot forget what I felt,

Bouts of energy being infused in me,
My limbs floating free,
As if my body wanted to try,
If it could still fly,
There is a connection between his and my soul,
Maybe we share a common goal,
The urge to fly I cannot deny,
Who will make me soar high?
Flying is the word, and flying is the connection,
Flying is our association.
Yes, he will wake when he can fly,

Anika kept repeating the lines in her mind and wondered how a human being could fly. The memory of Lady Carol gave her the answer. She thought, *If Lady Carol can fly, then maybe this prince too has the ability to fly.*

The memory of Lady Carol formed an association in her mind. She thought *is this prince Leo? He is also around fourteen years old and has blue eyes.*

Anika told Frederick, 'Creo que este chico es Leo.' [I think this boy is Leo.]

Frederick looked at the boy in surprise. He said, 'Él es Leo, el hijo de Drudan y Pajaro?' [He is Leo, the son of Drudan and Pajaro?]

Anika nodded and said, '¡Sí, creo que sí!' [Yes, I think so.]

She also told Frederick that she felt the solution to wake the prince was connected with his ability to fly. They waited for the birds to return with wood to energize the dwindling flame. It was pitch-dark everywhere. After sometime, they heard the chirping of birds. Frederick went out and waved at them. The birds flew inside the cave and one by one deposited twigs and branches of wood which they were holding in their beaks. Soon it was a huge pile of wood. Frederick immediately picked the burning twigs and placed them on the new pile of wood. The twigs carried by the birds were surprisingly dry and supported the fire to produce a huge flame. When there was fire and Anika and Frederick could see around, they were astounded to find thousands of birds sitting outside the cave. Some were carrying mangoes on their beaks, some apples, some cherries, and other fruits which Anika had never seen.

Anika came out and asked the red bird, 'My god! From where have these birds come?'

The red bird chirped, 'These are birds from every corner of the world and have carried the fruits to offer to the prince when he wakes.'

Anika told the red bird, 'I feel the prince will wake when he is able to fly.'

The red bird was alarmed. 'Our prince has been locked in this lake for years. I feel he has lost the strength to fly.'

Anika panicked. *How would the prince wake if he cannot fly?* She asked the bird, 'Is this prince Leo, the son of Drudan? Who locked the prince here?'

The red bird had tears in her eyes; she sadly replied, 'Yes, he is Leo. Drudan had locked him here.'

Anika could not believe what the red bird said and repeated the question, 'His father Drudan locked him here? How can a father be so cruel?'

The red bird wept and wept. She said, 'This little boy was only four years old when Drudan hit his mother Pajaro. Leo tried stopping Drudan and though he was only four years old, he stood in front of Drudan whose powers began to deplete as soon as he faced his son. Drudan howled in pain. Pajaro was breathing her last breath and told Leo to run to save his life. She was not sure if Leo could destroy Drudan's powers then. Poor boy Leo turned his back towards Drudan to run. Drudan immediately summoned the violet light to capture him. Violet entered Leo's veins but could not kill him, just paralyzed him. Drudan made several attempts to kill Leo. When he could not, he concealed his son in this glacial region. Leo has been lying here since then, absolutely paralyzed.'

Anika was shocked to hear that. 'This boy is paralyzed!' she exclaimed

The red bird grimly replied, 'Yes, he cannot move a limb. He belongs to the kingdom of clouds. He belongs to the special clan of human beings who can walk as well as fly but it is his dire fate; he cannot even lift a finger!'

Anika's mind was running. Something within was telling her that she was destined to meet Leo. Her heart refused to believe that Leo would not be able to fly. She thought –

She was born to influence the stars and planets to end the evil rule of Drudan. Leo was Drudan's son who was concealed in a glacier in Siepra Nevada. Frederick was cursed and banished to Siepra Nevada. Her mother Sussaina had sent Frederick to meet her in Shillong in India. The angel birds assisted Frederick in this. These were the same Angel birds who had been following Leo and protecting him. That means Sussaina knew where Leo was, and she knew that Frederick had not disappeared but had been cursed and banished to Siepra Nevada. How did her mother know about these events when she had lost all her powers? Anika continued to think. She felt her mother had been connecting all of them. She felt

Sussaina still had some powers with which she was monitoring their activities and leading them.

The loud chirping of birds made Anika come back from her reverie. She saw the birds had made a line and were taking turns to see the prince, offering whatever they had brought with them. Both Anika and Frederick made the prince sit near the fire so that he could feel the warmth. Anika was exhausted by the day's errands and slowly dozed off to sleep beside Leo.

She was suddenly woken by the erratic chirping of the birds. She went outside to check what the matter was and almost exclaimed at the sight. The sky was lined by a violet gleam, and Frederick was lying on his back. The red bird cried aloud, 'Anika, run inside, the violet light is approaching. It is coming again to capture the prince. Frederick has been hit by the light!'

Horrified, Anika began to think fast. *What should I do now?* The bird chirped loudly, 'We will form a cloud beneath the sky and stop the violet light from penetrating us.'

Anika screamed, 'No, you will die!'

The red bird said, 'We can give our life a hundred times to save the prince!'

Anika replied, 'No, it is my turn to save you. Please tell me what can stop the violet light.'

The red bird said, 'The tangent rays of the Sun. But this is a cursed region and has never seen a sunrise.'

Anika closed her eyes, joined her hands, and sat facing the sky. She chanted,

Oṃ bhūr bhuvaḥ svaḥ
tát savitúr váreṇ(i)yaṃ

bhárgo devásya dhīmahi
dhíyo yó naḥ pracodáyāt

The red bird alerted Anika, 'Save yourself, girl. What are you doing?'

Anika reverted, 'I do not know how to call the Sun. but my mother in India used to recite this prayer facing the Sun every morning. She told me it is one of the most powerful prayers. I am trying, maybe I can influence the Sun to rise.'

The red bird watched her for some time. The sky was turning violet with no sign of a sunrise.

The red bird chirped aloud, ordering the birds to form a cover over Anika, the prince, and Frederick.

Anika had closed her eyes and was praying aloud. The birds began to cry as they formed a cloud. They knew it was the last day of their life.

The sky got inundated with a noxious laughter. Drudan was sitting on his bee, and violet light was circling around him. He yelled, 'Violet, kill them all. Not a soul to be spared!'

Anika continued to recite the prayer. Her soul was calling the Sun to rise. There was no response from the sky, and yet she continued with her heart and mind focusing on the prayer to the Sun. She heard the boisterous laughter, but she prayed aloud. After a while, she heard another loud laughter from the sky and then painful chirping. She looked up and saw Drudan on the bee. The violet light was slowly spreading over the birds and killing them one by one. Anika yelled aloud, 'Oh, God, thou art the giver of life. May we receive thy supreme sin-destroying light!'

Drudan's voice echoed, 'When I did not spare my son, how will you escape death on a borrowed soul, darling Anika? I have left Frederick to live so that he can narrate how I killed you and Leo. No one dare come again to end my rule. Frederick, wake and see death. My dear Anika, don't waste time. This is a cursed land, and I rule here. Let the Sun sleep behind the clouds.'

Drudan looked at Frederick and sent a smoke-like ray towards him. 'Wake up, you fool.'

Frederick woke up with an excruciating pain arising in his limbs. He tried standing up but fumbled and fell.

The birds were trembling, the mountains shook violently, and the earth quaked with a thunderous sound. Drudan descended on his bee and entered the cave. He told Violet to pick the prince. Violet circled around Leo and lifted him in the air. Then Drudan came out of the cave and voiced aloud, 'Oh son, I wish you were like me. You are too good to be my blood!'

He looked at him venomously and said, 'I locked you so that you could continue living. Which father would want to kill his son? But alas, your destiny got Anika here and now I am left with no option but to kill you!'

Drudan lifted his hands and said, 'Violet, I promised you the greatest treat ever. Drink the royal blood of my son.'

Anika was aghast and joined her hands and looked up at the sky; with all her might she screamed:

Oṃ bhūr bhuvaḥ svaḥ
tát savitúr váreṇ(i)yam
bhárgo devásya dhīmahi
dhíyo yó naḥ pracodáyāt

The clouds burst aloud and split, letting a yellow ray of light penetrate through them.

Anika broke down crying, 'Thank you, Sun, our father, our creator, our protector!'

Drudan yelled as the ray fell on his face. His complexion began to turn like ash as the ray spread. He held his face and howled in pain. The violet light dropped the prince. Drudan was terrified, and trembling he told the bee 'Up and away!'

The birds were astounded seeing the sight. Sunray had come in this cursed land. The snow began to melt into streams and rivers. Frederick rushed towards Anika and hugged her. His eyes were swollen and replete with tears. He picked the prince and carried him where the ray of light was touching the ground. As the light touched his forehead, the bluish tint from Leo's face began to diminish and got replaced by a pinkish glow. The Prince murmured, 'Water!'

Chapter 13

The Defeat

Vivian was leading the throng on the road. The entire Zynpagua seemed to be rallying behind him. He had spent the day teaching people how to fight with a sword. Then he had revealed his plan to capture Drudan. Everyone had a role to play in that. Vivian was to confront Drudan and engage him in a combat. The people had to attack him from behind, ensuring that his mouth was sealed first to restrict the violet light from coming out. Vivian had promised that he would face Drudan's spells with his counter spell. Drudan's magic would not be able to harm anyone. The people were ready to attack Drudan as soon as he returned, but Vivian had stopped them. He had insisted that until his sister Anika returns and is able to win the support of Sun and Mars, all their effort would be a waste, as the violet light would sooner or later engulf everyone. Thus the right time for the revolt would only be when Anika returns and is able to seek the support of Mars and the Sun.

The people had agreed. Everyone was given a sword for self-defence. Vivian had planned a practice session the next morning in which he was playing Drudan. He wanted to ensure that the people see how the magical spells were being used. Everything went off well, and Vivian was very confident that he would be able to capture Drudan. Vivian had hypnotized ministers and others who were unwilling to support him. They had been kept in the palace jail to avoid any kind of a threat.

The next day everyone assembled near the palace gates. The people were carrying swords, daggers, and anything they had in the name of a weapon. Vivian stood in front, addressing the crowd. Sachinth and his father were supporting him completely. The rehearsal to kill Drudan began. Everything was going as per the plan when one of the ministers exclaimed, 'Violet!'

Everyone looked up. Some people began to yell while the others ran towards their houses. The sky had turned purple. Drudan was seated on his bee high up in the sky, and Violet was rotating around him. From the ground it seemed like a high-powered electric current. Drudan violently chanted some spells and aimed them at the people. Some people changed into beasts, some others became statues. Vivian was quick enough to send counter spells to change them back to their original form. When Drudan realized that his vice spells were not working, he yelled, 'People of Zynpagua, you have one chance. Surrender or die. I am sending Violet to swallow you. Those who bow down now will be spared; others can offer themselves to Violet.'

Everyone, except Vivian, Sachinth, and his father bowed down. Vivian screamed at the top of his voice, 'People, don't be scared. I will bring down Drudan through my spells. Let us capture him first. Without his instructions, Violet will not do anything.'

But the people refused to listen to Vivian. They were shaking with fright. Drudan guffawed. 'Oh my god, they refuse to stand by you, dear Vivian?'

Drudan aimed the violet light towards Sachinth and his father. Vivian came in front. He forcibly made the minister and Sachinth bow down. Drudan saw Vivian and laughed aloud, 'You insect, the son of stupid Soto. You think you can face Violet? You think so?'

He turned to Violet and said, 'Violet, Violet, here is a special treat. This man has royal blood. Drink as much as you can and enjoy the taste. Delicious it will be, I can assure you.'

The violet rays came charging down and began to circle around Vivian. He tried attacking Violet through his spells but felt choked.

Drudan looked down with his half-burnt face and shouted again, 'What are you waiting for, Violet? Kill him!'

Violet began to circle closer to Vivian who was struggling to breathe.

Sussaina was restlessly seeing Vivian from the shadow of the Moon. She wanted to break all barriers and go and save her son. But she could not. She prayed to Venus to save her son from Drudan's torture. She knew that Venus had been influenced by Anika and would help.

A silver beam of light emitted from the heavens and fell on Violet. The voice said, 'No, Drudan, you cannot kill Vivian!'

The voice was coming from the bright sparkling star Venus. 'You can't kill Vivian. I have promised Anika that I would protect her family. Your violet rays cannot overpower my light.'

Drudan laughed and said, 'Oh really? Then why did you let Anika's soul die?'

Venus began to sparkle, and the voice became louder, 'Because I wanted Leo and Anika's souls to unite. Sun could only be impressed with their united souls'

Drudan was scared listening to Venus. He knew he had no power to fight the Sun and the stars. He voiced out, 'I thought the stars had boycotted Zynpagua?'

Venus's voice echoed from the firmament, 'Sussaina's virtuous daughter has returned. She has been able to influence me. She has been able to save Leo and call Sun to Siepra Nevada. The future of Zynpagua depends on her efforts. For now I warn you, do not kill Vivian.'

Drudan was petrified. He knew that the stars were rising and his powers were failing. His violet light did not have the power to break through the protective beam of Venus. He instructed Violet, 'Take Vivian to the palace jail!'

Venus continued to cast its protective beam around Vivian, but Drudan chanted some very strong vice spells. The violet light began to flicker, and then it circled around Vivian and pulled him away. Vivian's forehead began to bleed with the pressure with which Violet pulled him. Venus could have rescued Vivian but was bound by the oath to the Sun god. Every man has to fight for his survival. Vivian still needed to learn the art of facing Drudan. He could only be the king of Zynpagua when his powers become greater than Drudan's. For that he had to face Drudan's torture and come out victorious from it. He had to do it himself.

Drudan instructed his soldiers to whip the people of Zynpagua. They were denied food for two days. The people regretted supporting Vivian and swore that never again would they go against Drudan.

183

Vivian was kept in the weirdest jail. He was made to sit on a wooden plank hanging midair with freezing ice on his head and boiling water touching his feet. Drudan thought if he could not kill Vivian, he would torture him to death.

Due to Venus's protective beam Vivian could neither feel the heat on his foot nor the chill of ice on his head. He felt drained and weak though.

Sussaina was seeing her son from the shadow of Moon and feeling helpless. She knew now only Anika could rescue Vivian by impressing Sun and Mars. Sussaina had been following Anika and Frederick as well. She was glad that they were able to rescue Leo but time demanded more speed.

Sussaina's mind was running fast. She knew that Drudan would now engage in making the violet rays more powerful. His next aim would be to capture Anika. He had seen her influence the Sun in Siepra Nevada. He would be preparing the violet light for another assault. Sussaina wanted to escape the shadow of the Moon and reach out to her children. But she could not. Without the combined energy of Venus, Sun, and Mars, the shadow of the Moon could not be destroyed. Another thought made her restless. It was important that the Sun rose in Zynpagua soon or else her people would not survive. Drudan had cut their food supply. They were deprived of the sunlight, and without food they would last only for hours, not even for days.

She remembered the prediction of the Moon when Drudan had captured her. The Sun had been very angry with Sussaina for neglecting her kingdom. The stars had withdrawn favours from Zynpagua, and the Sun refused to rise there. Moon had felt sorry for Sussaina. It had then predicted that 'the Sun would rise only when two royal and pious human beings share their souls to free Zynpagua from evil hands. One of them would face years of torture. He could only be saved when his soulmate rescues him from the region cursed and unknown.'

Sussaina had followed the signs of nature and had come to know that her daughter was one of the soul mates and the other one was Leo.

She had also come to know that Frederick had been tricked by Drudan and banished to Siepra Nevada. Sussaina had been sending Frederick to meet Anika because she knew that Frederick's curse could only be absolved when the Sun would rise in Siepra Nevada. Sussaina knew that Leo had been concealed there and that if Frederick helps Anika reach Leo, his curse would be absolved. Sussaina was glad that so far she was able to unite Vivian, Anika, Frederick and Leo. But the challenge was to save her people from dying. She knew the Sun had to rise now. She did not want to hasten Anika. Little Anika had reached Siepra Nevada but was exhausted. She had been courageously facing all the hurdles to save Leo. Any information about Vivian would create panic in her mind. The most important task for Anika currently was to rescue Leo and impress Mars.

Sussaina became restless. Her mind was racing— *How to save Vivian?* She helplessly walked to and fro in her dark confines. What if Drudan created something more fatal that could counter Venus's beam?. Whom should she send to save Vivian till Anika returns?

'Lady Carol and Femina', their name instantly struck her. Yes, Lady Carol could come for his rescue. Sussaina cleared her throat and closed her eyes. Her mind began to search for the location of Lady Carol. She found her in the midst of the jungle. Femina was sitting beside her, crying profusely. They had come to know that

185

Vivian was captured. Drudan's youngest queen also sat beneath a tree, trembling with fear. Sussaina instantly knew that she had to encourage them to be bold. She voiced aloud, 'Lady Carol!'

Femina and Lady Carol stood up when they heard the voice. They looked around but could not see anything. Then Sussaina spoke again, 'Lady Carol!'

Lady Carol looked up and stared at the sky. She said, 'Sussaina, is that you?'

Femina also jumped forward and murmured, 'Mother?'

Sussaina responded, 'Yes, it is me.'

Lady Carol asked Sussaina, 'Are you fine?'

'Don't worry about me, Lady. I have a favour to ask,' said Sussaina.

Lady Carol spoke out, 'Tell me, Sussaina, my life is for you.'

Sussaina began to weep and said, 'Lady, your daughter, Pajaro, has already sacrificed her life for me. Don't make me feel guilty.'

Lady Carol also began to cry and said, 'Sussaina, don't blame yourself, darling. It wasn't your fault.'

Sussaina was sobbing. 'It is my fault entirely, Lady. I trusted Drudan. He deceived us. The people of Zynpagua are suffering due to my negligence. It is my gross mistake. I am paying for my sins!'

Lady Carol tried comforting Sussaina, 'Don't worry, darling. We will see better days.'

Sussaina wiped her tears and said, 'Yes, I wish. Lady. I have good news for you. Anika has found Leo and has rescued him.'

Lady Carol was overjoyed to hear that. Sussaina continued, 'Leo is very fragile and unconscious. It will take him time to return to Zynpagua.'

Lady Carol listened attentively and said 'go on'.

'My son, Vivian, has to be saved from Drudan. While Venus is sending its protective beam, I am worried that Drudan might scientifically create something to destroy the beam. While I will do my best to reach out to Anika and Leo and tell them to hasten, you have to distract Drudan. Please ensure he gets no time to do his scientific research.'

Lady Carol instantly responded, 'Don't worry, Sussaina, I will.'

Sussaina thanked Lady Carol and then told Femina, 'Dear daughter, you reach out to the people of Zynpagua. Give them food and give them hope. Fight the soldiers and make the people fearless. Anika, Frederick, and Leo are returning. They need a valiant army to support them in their fight against Drudan. The stars get impressed when they see real effort coming from people. Mars for sure can never be impressed if people remain timid. Do your best to create an army. Vivian has been captured; it is your turn now to bring out valour in our people!'

Femina wiped her tears and, like a true warrior, said, 'I will ensure an army is created before Anika's return.'

'Dear Lady Carol, thank you for being with my children,' said Sussaina and then her voice faded.

Lady Carol and Femina continued to gape at the sky. When they did not hear Sussaina's voice again, they sat down to make a plan.

As per the plan, Lady Carol would enter Drudan's laboratory and distract him. Femina on the other hand, would ride on her horse and reach the well. The youngest queen was to accompany Femina. She would request the women there to support her. Lady Carol had insisted that Femina goes on a horse so that she could ride back with speed in case of any threat. Lady Carol had protected the jungle area with her spells. Lady Carol then chanted a spell. A huge pomegranate appeared in her hand. She handed it to Femina and said, 'Each grain of this pomegranate can fill the stomach of a person for a day. Feed the people of Zynpagua with it.'

She hugged Femina and the youngest queen and said, 'Best of luck, my girls, I am leaving now.' Saying that, she rose high in the sky and flew away.

Drudan was restlessly boiling a mixture on the flame when Lady Carol sneaked in his laboratory. This was the place where Drudan had worked for years to create the violet rays. After continuous experimenting he had discovered that Violet grew stronger by fresh blood of human being. Now, Drudan was trying to find a solution to dissolve Venus's beam. He was desperate to kill Vivian.

Lady Carol made herself invisible through a spell known only to the royal clan of the kingdom of clouds. As Lady Carol stepped in, Drudan looked up in suspicion. He sensed someone around and yelled, 'Who is there?'

Lady Carol stopped her breath. Drudan took deep breaths but could not trace anyone. He got back to work and began mixing two solutions. Then he opened another box which had a glowing beam in it and poured the solution on it. The glow from the beam began to diminish, and dissolved. Drudan laughed maliciously and said, 'My dear Venus, your beam will no longer be able to protect Vivian. Poor boy is going to die.'

Lady Carol trembled as she heard that. *Had Drudan found a solution to dissolve Venus's beam?* She instantly stepped forward and picked the bottle that contained the liquid and poured it on the floor.

'No!' screamed Drudan. 'Who did this?'

He looked around and began to take deep breaths. Lady Carol could not control her breath for long and soon Drudan sensed an intrusion. He murmured something and raised his hand to activate evil magic. Everything in the room began to rotate, including Lady Carol. She was spinning so fast that her head hurt and she could not move a limb to send a counter spell. Drudan calmly said, 'Whoever is here, come forward, or else I will spin you till you die.'

Lady Carol had begun to feel weak. She could not hold on to her invisible spell and appeared in front of Drudan.

On seeing her, he laughed, 'My dear mother-in-law, you are here! What an unpleasant sight. I have been missing you for years. Where did you disappear?'

'I did not want to look at your ugly face, Drudan,' said Lady Carol.

Drudan laughed hysterically and said, 'Then why are you here now?'

'To see your end,' said Lady Carol, smirking at Drudan.

Drudan stiffened and narrowed his eyes. His face turned stony, and his dark pale eyes began to look reddish. In a fit of anger, he picked a white jar and said 'Die!' and threw the liquid in it on Lady Carol.

Lady Carol instantly moved back but fell on the ground and hurt her leg. The liquid fell a few inches from her. Drudan guffawed. 'That was water.' He laughed again and said, 'Water broke your leg, Mom-in-law! Oops!'

Lady Carol tried getting up but could not. She had cut her thigh which began to bleed.

Drudan laughed again and said, 'First it was Vivian, and now it is you. Feeble insects. Whom should I kill first? Mom-in-law, I guess it should be an easy choice. I will kill Vivian and see your reaction.'

'How will you kill Vivian when I have spilled your solution,' asked Lady Carol, still struggling to get up.

Drudan looked at her angrily and said, 'Then I will kill Leo.'

Lady Carol yelled, 'You cannot even face him. Don't you remember all your evil powers were destroyed in his presence. You wriggled like a worm'

He laughed hysterically and said, 'You are right, I will not kill him. The people of Zynpagua will kill him. I have asked my soldiers to spread the news that the ghost of Frederick and Leo are haunting Zynpagua. These ghosts have to be burnt alive to save Zynpagua from disaster. You know how stupid these people are. They will believe in whatever I say.

Lady Carol knew the people of Zynpagua were highly superstitious and follow Drudan's instructions blindly. She became speechless.

Drudan in the meanwhile continued to laugh and smirk at her. He told her that Vivian would die soon while the people of Zynpagua would kill Leo and Frederick.

Drudan's mocking infuriated Lady Carol and she yelled, 'Anika has impressed the Sun at Siepra Nevada and is returning. She will come back and save everyone.'

Drudan knew Lady Carol was right. It took him a week to create the solution to dissolve Venus's beam, and now he would have to do it again. What if Anika returns by then? In a fit of rage, he asked his soldiers to arrest Lady Carol and lock her in the jail.

Chapter 14

Freedom from Curse

Frederick pulled out a bottle of water from his bag and made the prince sip it. The prince opened his eyes and looked around. Anika was so mesmerized with his looks that she simply stood there awestruck.

The birds outside began to chirp again. One of the birds carried a pomegranate and handed it to Leo. 'Dear prince, please eat it and give us the seeds. We will plant these seeds everywhere to grow trees.'

Leo slowly moved his hand and sat up. The sunray fell on his legs, and he gradually moved his limbs. The red bird began to weep and said, 'Our prince can move his limbs. He is no longer paralyzed! The Sun's ray has cured him!'

Leo looked at the red bird and said, 'My angel, thank you for protecting me for so many years.'

The red bird wept and said, 'My prince, it is wonderful to hear your voice. I am so grateful to the Sun and Anika.'

LEO

Leo looked at Anika and smiled. 'Thank you, Anika,' said he.

Anika got goose bumps, and she stammered to say, 'Mention not!'

Then the prince bit into the pomegranate and exclaimed, 'It is so delicious!'

The red bird suggested, 'Dear prince spit out the seeds!' Leo did as he was told. The birds collected the seeds in their beak and flew out, planting the seeds in the region.

The red bird flew towards Frederick and said, 'We have started the process of absolving your curse. However, the Sun has to rise and set every day for trees to grow and birds to reside. Dear Anika, Sun has sent a ray, please pray to the Sun to have mercy on this region.'

Anika nodded. She sat in front of the ray of the Sun and prayed.

Sun, our Father,
The source of all life,
Relieve us from our plight,
Send us shining light.

Anika went on calling the Sun but nothing happened. She looked at Frederick who sat in one corner, dejected and sad. He told Anika, 'My curse can never be absolved!'

Anika tried again and failed. The Sun continued to send only one ray.

The red bird flew very close to Anika and said, 'Dear Anika, cry out the pain in your heart. Let the Sun know what you have been going through.'

Anika was silent for some time and then sang the song,

193

My mother is locked behind the Moon,
My brother can be captured soon,
My uncle is trapped in a curse,
Could destiny have it worse?
My father is where I do not know,
Send us your blissful glow,
Enlighten our mind and brighten our land,
Come, dear Sun,
Rise in this land.

As Anika finished her song, a clear blue firmament could be seen replacing the dense fog and then the Sun rose, soaring high in the east. The birds danced merrily, and Frederick jumped with joy. Anika stood there with her hands joined and gaze fixed on the Sun. Tears were rolling out from her eyes continuously. Weeping she sat down and bowed before the Sun.

Then a thought made Anika stand up and pray to the Sun, 'Dear Sun, thank you for rising and saving us. Please pardon the curse of Zynpagua and rise there. Our people are ailing and dying.'

There was no response and Anika did not know how else to address the Sun god. When she was about to repeat her words, a loud heavenly voice said, 'I will come to Zynpagua when the time is right. Continue your fight against evil Drudan, dear daughter. I will come when the time is right.'

A ray of the Sun fell on Anika's forehead. She felt a surge of energy in her as if she had never been tired. She bowed to the Sun in gratitude. The Siepra Nevada region got inundated with blissful sunshine. Birds from far and wide began coming to the region, carrying seeds in their beaks. As soon as they placed the seeds on the ground, it germinated into a plant and quickly grew to become trees.

The birds started singing in unison.

Our dear prince has come,
Rescued from the evil one,
The Sun has sent its virtuous rays,
Gone are the ugly days.

Other birds flew near Anika, carrying fruits, offering them to her and then flying off with the seeds, determined to make the place worth living.

The red bird danced in the sky and came and sat on Anika's shoulders. 'My princess, this region has not seen the Sun since ages. Thank you for cajoling the Sun to bless our land. With the Sun's blessing, we will flood this region with trees and plants and ensure it is worth living. Thank you, our saviour!'

Anika was speaking to the red bird when she noticed two white peacocks flying very close to the ground. They came near Anika and spread their wings and danced. One of them hopped towards Frederick and pecked on his forehead thrice. Frederick grimaced and said, 'What are you doing?'

Anika was surprised as Frederick spoke English. Then the second peacock came forward and said, 'Frederick, your curse is absolved. Go- live a free life wherever you want. Your purpose is fulfilled.'

Frederick began to weep. He bowed before the peacocks and said, 'Pardon me for all my sins.'

The peacocks sat on Frederick's shoulders and said, 'The peacocks you tried killing had not died, they are still alive. They are our parents. They live happily in the kingdom of clouds. You have paid for your sins. You are free now!'

Before Frederick could say anything, the two peacocks soared little above the ground and disappeared.

Anika ran towards Frederick and hugged him, 'Uncle, you are free now. Let us all go back to Zynpagua and save our mother!'

Frederick lifted Anika in his arms and danced with joy. The red bird insisted that they should first celebrate this moment of happiness.

Two birds descended from the sky carrying a crown of flowers. They merrily placed it on Anika's head and sang the song:

Our dear prince has come,
Rescued from the evil one,
The Sun has sent his virtuous rays,
Gone are the ugly days.

Frederick and Leo joined the celebration. While dancing, Leo held Anika's hand. She was mesmerized by Leo's charm and did not know how to react.

Leo was dancing in a circle with the birds and came closer to Anika and said, 'Thank you, Anika, for saving my life. I knew you would come one day.'

Anika was surprised to hear that. 'You knew? How?'

Leo gently smiled and said, 'Aunt Sussaina has been calling out to me. She kept telling me that my saviour would come one day. I would have died long time back, but she continued to wake me and promise me that I would have a very long life.'

Anika was taken aback to hear that. Did her mother know about their future? She marvelled at the way her mother had built hope in everyone, despite being confined in the shadow of the Moon.

Leo smiled gently once again and said, 'Anika, let us dance today. Please don't think about anything. We do not know how difficult the future is going to be.

Frederick pushed Anika ahead, and she commenced dancing with Leo and Frederick on each side. They hopped forward and backwards, with their legs swinging in unison.

As they continued to dance, Vivian's face flashed in front of Anika's eyes. She saw him bleeding and wounded.

Anika yelled aloud and said, 'We have to leave now. My brother, Vivian, is in danger!'

Everyone stopped and came close to Anika. Frederick asked her "What happened?"

She said "I saw Vivian injured and bleeding. We have to help him"

Leo agreed with Anika and said "Let us leave right away"

The seven birds circled around the three of them and bid adieu. The red bird said, 'We will always be there to help you. For now, we are leaving for the kingdom of clouds but will continue to visit you. This region has become beautiful and lovely, and we birds will be grateful to you forever.!'

While the seven birds flew away, Siepra Nevada region looked stunning with the brilliant Sun, green trees, and numerous birds.

Anika, Vivian, and Leo waved goodbye to the birds and got ready to leave. She looked at the sky to call Venus, but Leo stopped her and said, 'I can fly. Hold my hand and I will take you and Frederick to Zynpagua.'

Anika smiled and hesitatingly gave her hand to Leo. He held Anika's hand on the right and Frederick's hand on the left and instructed them, 'I will lift you up in the air. Once we are floating, continue moving your legs forward and backward till I have gained speed. You can stop once I start flying very high.'

Anika was very nervous and asked Leo, 'How can you fly? You have no wings.'

Leo laughed and said, 'We fly from our mind. We control our body through our mind and command it to lift itself. This is a special quality of people from the kingdom of clouds. All of us can fly. Let us not waste time, Anika, hold my hand.'

Anika caught Leo's hand tightly while Frederick held the other. Leo closed his eyes and commanded 'Up!'

The three were floating in midair when Anika screamed.

The image of Vivian appeared again. He was standing on fire and everything around was burning. Anika told Leo to hurry. Leo gained speed, and in no time they entered Zynpagua and landed in the jungle. The fisherman was sitting there, worried and restless. He told them what had transpired in Anika's absence. Anika was shocked to learn that Vivian had been captured and that Lady Carol and Femina had not returned since last two days.

Frederick, Leo, and Anika instantly left the jungle to rescue Vivian. They were walking in the streets when one of the commoners recognized Frederick and Leo. He ran away saying, 'The ghosts have arrived!'

Before Leo, Anika, and Frederick could understand anything, the commoner returned with a crowd which was carrying fire torches with them. One of them screamed, 'Kill the ghosts!'

They charged towards the three. Leo quickly held Anika's and Frederick's hand and lifted them up in the air. Another member in the crowd yelled, 'Oh my god, they are flying. They will kill us!' The crowd yelled unanimously, 'Kill them!'

Anika requested Leo to descend. When they came back to the ground, Anika tried telling the people that they had come to rescue Zynpagua from Drudan. The commotion around was so loud that her voice got subdued in that. They began throwing stones at Frederick and Leo. The soldiers got alerted as well. They charged towards Frederick and captured him. Leo got pulled by the crowd, and they began to beat him.

Someone came from behind and handcuffed Anika. On turning around, she saw an army of twelve soldiers standing behind her. One of them commanded, 'Take her to the king!'

The second soldier came closer to Anika and as he pulled her, someone struck him with a sword. The soldier yelled in pain and retreated. On looking up, Anika saw Femina with a group of five women, mounted on horses. Femina pushed the soldiers away, and then her little army defeated them.

The soldiers got injured and fainted.

Femina then dismounted the horse and hugged Anika dearly and said 'Thank God you are safe!

She looked at Leo and Frederick and greeted them. Turning to Anika, she continued, 'Vivian has been captured, and the entire Zynpagua had been instigated against the three of you. I suggest you go to the jungle and make a plan. Without impressing the Sun and Mars, none of us would be able to defeat Drudan.'

Anika nodded and told Leo, 'Let us leave.'

She hugged Femina and said, 'You are a fearless warrior. Take care of yourself. I love you!'

Femina had tears in her eyes as she kissed Anika on the forehead and said, 'I love you too!'

As Femina kissed Anika, a flash appeared in front of Anika's eyes. She saw Femina in the form of a statue. A very young girl was standing near Femina. The girl was wearing her school uniform with a name tag of Aarna Malhotra. She had an electronic gadget in her hand with which she was trying to bring Femina back to life.

Anika murmured 'Femina, what happened to you? Who is she?'

A loud voice got Anika back from her reverie. Frederick was shaking Anika. He asked her 'What happened? Whom were you speaking to?'

Anika instantly asked 'Where is Femina? What happened to her?'

Femina was standing beside Frederick and said 'I am here Anika. What happened, why were you calling my name?'

Anika was taken aback. She thought *why did she see Femina like a statue?*

Leo placed his hand on Anika's shoulders and said 'Anika, I think you were day dreaming. Let us leave now'

Anika nodded and left for the jungle with Frederick and Leo, leaving Femina and her little army in Zynpagua.

They reached the jungle and sat down to make a plan. The sensation of the buzzing bee made Anika realize that Sussaina was trying to call her.

Anika looked up and said 'Mother Sussaina, is that you?'

Sussaina's voice was trembling as she told Anika, 'Hurry and save Vivian!'

'Mother Sussaina, where are you?' asked Anika.

'Anika, please do not ask me anything. Leo, my child, please take Anika and Frederick to the palace. Vivian's life is in danger!'

Leo assured Sussaina, 'Aunt Sussaina, don't worry, we will leave right now!'

When Sussaina's voice could not be heard anymore, Leo took Anika and Frederick to the palace. On reaching the gates of the palace, they were shocked to see the area flooded with people. A violet glow was hovering in the air. As they came closer, they saw Vivian tied to a tree. Drudan was standing beside him and saying, 'I have destroyed the protective beam of Venus. Even the stars cannot save this chap of Sussaina. She was a wicked woman who had displeased the stars. I am going to kill Vivian!' Then pointing to the crowd, Drudan yelled, 'You will kill Frederick and Leo. I know Leo is my son, but he died years back. We cannot afford to have ghosts in Zynpagua. People, I want you to burn the ghosts or you will not survive!'

Anika was shocked to see that people of Zynpagua believed in ghosts. They were primitive, and Drudan had sapped their wisdom.

The people of Zynpagua voiced in unison, 'We will burn the ghost of Frederick and Leo.'

Advancing towards Vivian, Drudan yelled, 'I will initiate the process of cleansing Zynpagua. This boy here has vile blood. See!' Saying this, Drudan slit Vivian's shoulders. A gush of blood oozed out.

Vivian yelled, 'Drudan, you wicked man, don't fool the people!'

Drudan laughed and said, 'No boy, I am not fooling the people, I am ensuring they understand the difference between virtue and vice!'

Drudan then pulled a dagger and, aiming at Vivian, yelled, 'I will drain out blood from his heart.'

When Drudan was about to pierce the dagger in Vivian's heart, Leo came and stood in front of him. Drudan yelled, 'No!' and lost all his strength. Unable to stand, he sat down and wriggled like a worm.

Leo spoke calmly, 'I hate to call you my father. You are such an evil man.'

Drudan pleaded, 'Leo, my son, move away from me!'

'No, Father, your place is in the dungeons.'

Drudan looked up in the sky. The violet light was circling high above. He garnered his strength, slowly raised his hand and pointing towards Leo, said, 'Violet, come and swallow him!'

The purple glow which was circling on the sky changed into lightning and came charging towards Leo. Frederick dashed in front pulling Leo behind. The violet light had no time to change its direction and entered Frederick's body. Frederick gasped for breath twice and then fell. Leo held him before he touched the ground. Frederick had turned cold, and was not breathing. Anika ran towards Frederick and began to rub his hand. But there was no response from him.

She asked Leo nervously, 'Why is he not responding?'

Leo could not brace courage to tell Anika that Frederick was no more. He simply placed his hand on Anika's shoulder. The expression on his face plainly told Anika that Frederick had died. In a state of shock, Anika continued to gape at Frederick.

Drudan slowly dragged himself away from Leo when he was preoccupied in attending to Frederick. Gaining his strength, Drudan yelled, 'Violet, you have killed Frederick, now finish Vivian!'

Violet pulled itself out of Frederick's heart and, with a speed of lightning, went in the direction of Vivian. Seeing this, Anika howled, 'No, save my brother!'

Drudan laughed aloud. 'Next is your turn insect!'

Anika began to weep. She closed her eyes and prayed, 'Sun, my father, give us your divine light.'

She opened her eyes and saw Violet circling around Vivian.

Drudan was laughing hysterically and said, 'Don't waste time. Enter his heart and drink his blood. He is yours.'

The violet light began to straighten in front of Vivian's heart. Drudan voiced again, 'Hurry up, there are two more to go!'

Leo ran to save Vivian while Anika closed her eyes and repeated, 'Sun, my father, send your divine light!'

When Anika opened her eyes, she saw violet rays circling around Leo.

Drudan was yelling and saying, 'Violet, don't waste time on Leo, hit Vivian first!'

Vivian saw Anika running towards him. He tried stopping her and said, 'Runaway, my dear sister, run as fast as you can!'

As Violet circled closer to Vivian, his voice gradually faded. Anika saw Vivian collapsing under pressure of violet rays.

She immediately sat on her knees and looking at the sky she repeated the words

'Oṃ bhūr bhuvaḥ svaḥ
tát savitúr váreṇ(i)yaṃ
bhárgo devásya dhīmahi
dhíyo yó naḥ pracodáyāt'

A thunderous echo made everyone look up at the sky. The clouds were splitting, but there was no sign of the Sun.

Anika began to tremble; she repeated, 'Dear Sun, our saviour, you promised to send your divine light. Please save my brother!'

Vivian's shriek made Anika turn towards him. The violet rays had hit his heart; with another gasp of breath Vivian lost consciousness. Violet was about to enter his body when Anika heard the people scream, 'The Sun! The Sun!'

The darkness of Zynpagua faded in seconds, as the brilliant yellow rays penetrated through the sky and the milieu got showered with brilliant sunlight. The people of Zynpagua jumped with joy as if each ray of the Sun gave them strength after years. Their body began to straighten, and their faces brightened.

As the rays of Sun fell on violet light, flames could be seen erupting from it and the violet rays dissolved in dust.

Drudan was aghast seeing the sight. The Sun had risen, destroying his precious violet light. That was his only weapon.

From the horizon a slanting ray came and fell on Vivian's heart. Anika turned around to see the Sun shining in the east.

Drudan's skin turned charcoal as the sunrays fell on him. He pulled out his dagger and ran towards Vivian. Leo held Drudan's hand and pushed him back. Drudan fell powerlessly. Leo was about to attack Drudan when he screamed, 'You will lose your grandmother Carol, if you kill me. I have bound her by the spell of my life. If I die, she will die as well!'

Leo stepped back and asked Drudan, 'Where is my grandmother?'

Drudan said, 'I will not tell you. First let me escape!'

Leo was puzzled. How could he let Drudan escape?

'Step back, son, move away from me or else I will kill Carol!'

Leo retreated.

Drudan pulled out the crimson handkerchief from his pocket and waved it in the air, 'Come fast, my crimson bee.' Said he

A huge bee appeared instantly, and Drudan sat on it to escape. His skin was burning with the sunrays. He flew up in the air and disappeared.

Chapter 15

The Rays of Stars

As Drudan escaped, he called out, 'Leo, you can never find your grandmother!' Leo knew his father was a cheat. He cried out 'Run wicked man, run or else I will kill you.' Drudan instructed his bee to hasten and was soon out of sight.

Leo ran back to help Anika, who was sitting beside Vivian, trying to wake him. Before Leo could say anything to her, he heard loud screaming. Anika and Leo looked up and saw Femina, the youngest queen, and Lady Carol tied with ropes, locked in a cage. Drudan had hung them in midair. He was seated on his bee, holding an umbrella, to avoid the rays of the Sun.

Drudan yelled, 'People of Zynpagua, you have last chance to save yourself. Capture Vivian, Leo, and Anika and surrender them to me. You can see these three women. They are going to meet their death soon. People save yourself!'

The people gaped at Drudan absolutely awestruck. Femina yelled out from the cage, 'People, you have the sunlight now. You have also gained strength. Don't listen to Drudan. Capture him!'

Drudan got furious listening to Femina and said 'You want to check my strength? Look!'

He murmured something and pointed his finger towards Femina and said, 'Spell of hell, take her life and make her stone!'

Femina turned into a statue. Drudan laughed venomously while Anika and Leo watched in horror. Leo asked Anika, 'What should we do now?'

Anika was trembling. She said, 'Drudan's powers can only be destroyed when the sunrays get combined with those of Venus and Mars. I have impressed Venus and the Sun but do not know how to influence Mars.'

Leo told her, 'Anika, I will face Drudan. You please go and find a way to impress Mars. Vivian is still unconscious, and we do not know magic to combat Drudan's magical spells!'

Anika agreed with Leo. Drudan was watching them and said, 'Leo and Anika, surrender now!'

Leo raised his hand and flew up, facing Drudan directly. Drudan fumed 'Go away, you horrible son born from a treacherous woman, go away!'

Leo went closer. Drudan began to shake and lost the grip of the cage which had Lady Carol, Femina's statue, and the youngest queen. The cage began to fall from the sky. Leo left Drudan and flew down to hold the cage. He balanced the cage on his shoulders and descended to the ground. Then he placed it carefully on the floor.

Drudan knew that the only way to conquer Zynpagua was to reach the shadow of the Moon and capture Sussaina. His violet rays were destroyed. He knew he could rule Zynpagua if Sussaina was in his custody. He whispered, 'My crimson bee, let us secretly flee!' The bee vibrated its wings aggressively, prepared to cover a great distance in seconds. Drudan held the bee tightly as it soared higher and higher towards the shadow of the Moon.

In the meanwhile Anika had dragged Vivian towards a secluded corner and was trying to think of a way to impress Mars. Frederick was lying dead in close proximity. Seeing him, Anika began to howl and could not focus.

She sat down and prayed to Venus, 'Dear Venus, please show me a way to bring back my uncle's life.' Venus began to sparkle in the sky. It transformed into a beautiful lady with white shining clothes. She descended from the clouds and came and sat beside Anika who was weeping profusely. Anika put her head on Venus's feet and asked her for help.

Venus replied, 'Frederick died while saving Leo. Mars can revive a person who has died sacrificing his life. Pray to Mars!'

Before Anika could thank Venus, she disappeared.

Anika joined her hands and faced the sky, which looked bright and sunny. She tried various prayers, but they did not work. She tried reading the symbol of nature but failed to interpret anything. Seeing Frederick lying dead overwhelmed her with grief. She was unable to think. In the meanwhile one of the commoners came forward and said, 'Dear princess, your uncle's heart has stopped beating. He should be cremated'

Anika yelled at the man, 'Don't touch him. He will live, he has to live!'

She looked up at the sky and said, 'I do not know how to impress you dear Mars. Please use your powers and save my uncle Frederick. We need him.'

She was going through a terrible sinking feeling when she heard Leo call out 'Anika, do you know how we can open this cage?'

Anika turned around and saw Lady Carol and the youngest queen wounded and Femina turned to stone. She felt helpless and covered her face to stop the tears trickling down her cheeks. Leo came closer and assured her, 'Anika, please think of a way to impress Mars, then everything will be fine.'

The people of Zynpagua came in groups to hail and bow before Anika for impressing the Sun. They rejoiced that their princess was back and had saved them.

Lady Carol cried out "Leo my child, my little baby, come here my son". Leo ran towards Lady Carol and said 'Grandma, my lovely grandma!' He wanted to hug Lady Carol but she was still locked in the cage. Lady Carol saw Leo and said 'Step back son, I will try breaking the lock.' She placed her finger on the lock and said 'tic tic, break it.'

The lock rotated and split open. Leo hurriedly opened the cage and hugged his grandma dearly. After this, Leo placed Femina's statue safely in a secured corner and Lady Carol, Leo and the youngest queen went towards Anika.

Anika was sitting beside Frederick when she heard Sussaina's cry. 'Drudan, you know you can't kill me!'

Terrified, Anika looked around and asked Leo, 'Where is Drudan?'

Leo could not see Drudan anywhere. He flew up to check on Drudan but could not find him.

Then he heard a boisterous laughter. Drudan screamed, 'I am on the shadow of the Moon. Now, you insects listen to me or else you would see Sussaina paralyzed. I may not be able to kill her, but I can cast a spell and paralyze her!'

Anika yelled, 'Evil Drudan, leave my mother!'

Drudan laughed aloud. 'I am glad you know how evil I can be. Now listen to me. Ask my son Leo to carry Vivian and you here. Your mother needs company. This time, I will ensure that the three of you are tied here in the shadow of the Moon. This is my region! Only my evil spells work here. Leo, hurry and get Vivian and Anika or else your aunt Sussaina will be paralyzed!'

Sussaina cried aloud, 'Leo, don't listen to him! Stay there and save Vivian and Anika.'

Anika asserted desperately, 'No mother, we have to save you. Leo, please take us there!'

Drudan heard Anika and said, 'You are a wise girl. Before you leave Zynpagua, please tell those foolish people that they can have only one ruler, and that is me.'

Leo whispered, 'Anika, the shadow of the Moon is the place where evil resides. Even my powers will fail there. Drudan will spellbind us. You have to break the shadow. The Sun and Venus are happy with you, think fast on impressing Mars.'

Anika aggressively disagreed. 'No! Drudan will paralyze my mother. I have to go!'

Leo calmed Anika down and said, 'Drudan can only sense vibrations from the shadow of the Moon. I will take Vivian and fly. Drudan will wait as far as he knows we are approaching. You have to ensure that you are able to impress Mars in the meantime. We have to break the shadow or else we all are doomed.'

Anika refused to obey Leo. Lady Carol also advised Anika to follow what Leo was saying. She hugged Leo and said, 'My dear grandson, it is your turn now to save Sussaina.'

Leo smiled and said, 'I will do my best, grandma.'

Lady Carol then murmured the 'wake up' spell and brought Vivian back to consciousness.

Vivian was shocked to see Femina turn into a statue. He was furious and agreed with Leo on his plan. Thus Leo and Vivian left Anika with Lady Carol and proceeded towards the shadow of the Moon. Leo held Vivian and commanded 'Up and away!'

Soon they were seen flying high up in the air.

Anika sat quietly with her mind racing rapidly. The sight of dead Frederick burnt her soul. She faced the sky and said, 'Dear Mars, my family is dying. Please show me a way!'

Anika could hear the loud and boisterous laughter of Drudan. He was saying, 'Leo, you are a wise boy. Get Anika and Vivian fast.'

But after some time, Drudan was heard yelling, 'Where is Anika? You cheated me like your mother. You are trying to save Anika? Now you will bear the fruit of your treachery. I am sending fire to Zynpagua. Everyone out there deserves to die!'

Anika was stunned to hear Drudan. His voice was followed by Leo's and Vivian's angry voices. Sussaina was heard saying 'Stop it!'

Soon balls of fire were dropping from the sky. The people of Zynpagua were terrified and ran, yelling 'save us princess'. The fireballs began to drop sporadically, burning houses and trees. The entire region was lit with fire. Lady Carol tried producing water through her spells, but soon the intensity of heat was so much that she could not stand in front of it. She told Anika to run towards the river while she tried saving the people by creating a halo between them and the fire. Anika did not know what to do. She sat down in front of the flames and prayed,

Mars, please use your powers,
Unite with Sun and Venus,
Send your beneficial showers!

A huge ball of fire emerged before Anika and said, 'The people of Zynpagua can only be saved when a noble person sacrifices his life for the cause. I call upon the one who is ready to sacrifice his life for saving his people. Come forward!'

The people of Zynpagua backed out. The flame burnt fiercely and a voice said, 'Is there no one here as brave as fire?'

Anika observed the flame and asked, 'How do I know that the people of Zynpagua will be spared once the sacrifice is made?'

The fire flickered violently and said, 'I belong to Mars—the planet of valour. Show me your courage and I promise to spare your people!'

Anika looked up in the sky. She could faintly hear the voices of Sussaina and Vivian. She knew they were in trouble. She told the fire, 'I am ready to sacrifice my life, but please save the people of Zynpagua and rescue my mother, brother, and Leo from the shadow of the Moon.' Saying that, Anika closed her eyes, and taking a deep breath, jumped in the flames. Lady Carol tried stopping Anika, but she was late.

As Anika jumped in the fire, the flames were replaced by flowers. She was surprised at what had happened. She looked up and saw three beams uniting in midair. One was being emitted by the Sun, the other Venus, and the third from a new star with a reddish gleam that emerged in the sky. The flames everywhere were replaced by mild showers. The people of Zynpagua began to dance in the soothing milieu.

A sound from the new star emerged and said, 'Anika, I am Mars and am very pleased with you. I have united my powers with the Sun and Venus to destroy the shadow of the Moon.'

Anika began to weep and bowed down thanking the stars. The new star flickered with a reddish glow and said, 'Anika, I will grant you a wish. Ask for it!'

Before Anika could say anything, she saw Vivian and Leo descend from the clouds. They were holding Sussaina. Anika called out, 'Mother!'

Sussaina immediately told Anika, 'Listen to Mars!'

'Are you all right, Mother?' asked Anika.

Mars interrupted her and said, 'Anika, I cannot stay for long. Ask me for a wish now or lose the chance.'

Anika instantly bowed low before Mars and said, 'Please return my uncle Frederick's life!'

The red star flickered violently and sent its rays on Anika. They were very harsh and intense, making her skin turn red and she fainted.

When she woke up, she saw her mother caressing her forehead. Frederick was standing near her feet and rubbing them while Vivian and Leo were holding her hand. Anika was relieved to find everyone safe. She looked at Frederick and said, 'Uncle Frederick, you are alive?'

Frederick smiled and said, 'Mars granted you the wish. Thank you for saving my life. Muchas gracias!'(Thank you very much)

Sussaina gently smiled at Anika and said, 'Dear daughter, you have saved Zynpagua and have rescued me. My little darling, you have done it!'

A tear came rolling down her eyes. Anika asked Sussaina, 'Mother, you look very sad. What is the matter?'

Sussaina wiped her tears and said, 'Don't worry, darling.'

Anika looked around and saw the grim expression on Vivian's face as well. She asked him, 'What is the matter?'

Vivian tried smiling but instead began to howl. He said, 'Drudan has escaped. Before leaving, he told us that our father Soto is in his clutches. When we did not believe him, he showed us his image. He is somewhere in the deep sea, but where, we do not know!'

Anika instantly blurted out, 'Thank God, our father is alive!' She looked at Vivian and said, 'We can go and find him. Can we not?'

Vivian shook his head and sadly replied, 'No, we cannot go!'

'Why?' asked Anika, aghast.

He said, 'That is because Drudan has bound us with the statue of Femina. If we move out of Zynpagua, the statue will break!'

Anika could not believe what she heard. 'But can we not bring Femina back to life from a state of statue?'

Vivian began to weep. 'No, we have tried all possible magical spells, but Femina is not changing into human form!'

Anika insisted, 'No, it can't be, try again!'

Vivian cleared his throat and told Anika, 'There is another problem.'

Anika got tense and asked, 'What is it?'

'Before Drudan left, he pledged revenge on you. He said he would be attacking your Indian family on Earth.'

Anika was furious. 'No! He cannot do that. Let us go and save my family. I love them!'

Sussaina hugged Anika and said, 'I know, my dear daughter. Calm down. We cannot go. If any of us leaves, Femina's statue will break, and she will die!'

Anika began to cry and said, 'Mother, then what is the solution?'

Sussaina held Anika and said, 'Be brave, my girl. There is hope. Frederick had died when Drudan bound us with this spell. Drudan did not spell bind him. He can go to the Earth and get your family here!'

'But they will not come. In fact they will not believe Frederick. Vivian told me that they would continue to sleep till I am back. Why can we not let them sleep till I return.'

Sussaina held Anika's shoulder and said, 'Anika, it is important to wake them before Drudan reaches there or they will be attacked, absolutely aware. We will have to send Frederick. He will explain everything to them.'

Lady Carol also suggested 'Anika, people from the kingdom of clouds cannot be bound by the spell of connection. Thus Drudan could not bind me and Leo with Femina's statue. In case of any threat to your family in India, Leo and I will follow Frederick and ensure that they are safe.'

Anika had no choice but to agree with Sussaina and Lady Carol.

Sussaina went and stood on an elevation near the gates. She called out 'People of Zynpagua come closer'. The people began to crowd around Sussaina.

Sussaina announced, 'Vivian, my son, is your new king!'

The people clapped and said 'We welcome our new King. He is valiant indeed.'

Someone from the crowd yelled 'Will Princess Anika leave us and go?'

Sussaina smiled and said 'No, she will stay with us.'

Someone else from the crowd suggested 'Why can she not rule Zynpagua?'

Sussaina smiled again and said 'She is very young. Besides, she has a bigger challenge at hand. My people I cannot tell you her future but she is born to chase a different dream'

The people were satisfied that their Princess would stay in Zynpagua. Happy days were back again for them.

Sussaina's family was silently camouflaging their plight. Once the crowd dispersed, Vivian picked Femina's statue and kept it safely in the palace.

Frederick got ready to leave for the Earth. He promised Anika he would take care of her family in India.

Leo and Lady Carol bid adieu to Sussaina as the kingdom of clouds was without a ruler. They had to keep their kingdom safe from Drudan.

While Lady Carol and Sussaina bid farewell to each other, they knew that Leo and Anika were soul mates and could not be separated for long.

Destiny would continue to play its tricks to unite the soul mates.

With a mixed feeling of joy and sadness, everyone parted ways!

Book 2

Secrets of Zynpagua: Search of Soul mates.

Frederick reaches India but Anika's family refuse to trust him and gets him arrested. On not getting any news from Frederick, Sussaina calls Leo to Zynpagua and sends him to India. When Leo reaches India, he rescues Frederick and traces Drudan. Leo realizes that Drudan had strengthened his scientific powers. He had found the weaknesses of every planet and was using this knowledge to attack Zynpagua. Leo also discovers the only way to convert Femina back to human form was to find a 6 year old girl by the name of Aarna Malhotra. She was also known as the gadget girl who had the power to solve Drudan's technological formulas. Leo and Frederick set out to find Aarna Malhotra, absolutely unaware that Drudan had attacked Zynpagua by then.

Read

Secrets of Zynpagua: Search of Soul mates.

To discover the unusual circumstances in which Leo and Anika's souls unite to defeat Drudan.

Fun with Spanish

Hello: ¡hola! (h is silent when pronouncing Hola)

How are you?: ¿Cómo estás?

Very well, thank you: Muy bien, gracias.

Glad (to meet you): Mucho gusto.

Good Morning: ¡Buenos días!

Goodbye: ¡Adiós!

The Boy: El Chico

The Girl: La Chica

Beautiful: Bonito/Lindo

Pretty Girl: muchacha bonita (OR) chica linda

The Story: La Historia.

Nice: Bien.

The Dance: La Danza.

Song: La canción

Sing: Cantar

Character description

Anika: the Princess of Zynpagua, 10 years of age.

Sussaina: Anika's mother and the Queen of Zynpagua who is locked in the Shadow of Moon.

Frederick: Anika's uncle who has been banished to an Invisible land called Siepra Nevada near Spain.

He is 21 years old and speaks Spanish

Vivian: Anika's brother. He is 15 years old.

Femina: The most valorous girl in Zynpagua. She is 17 years old.

Leo: The missing son of Drudan, 14 years old.

Drudan: a malicious scientist who rules Zynpagua.